D1169627

The Bounty Hunter

A REBA 1 NOVEL

The Bounty Hunter

Marian Flandrick Bray

ZondervanPublishingHouse
Grand Rapids, Michigan

A Division of HarperCollinsPublishers

The Bounty Hunter
Copyright © 1992 by Marian Bray

Requests for information should be addressed to:
Zondervan Publishing House
Grand Rapids, Michigan 49530

Library of Congress Cataloging-in-Publication Data

Bray, Marian Flandrick, 1957–
    The bounty hunter / Marian Bray.
        p. cm.
    Summary: Although she knows that the wolverine invading her part of
the San Gabriel Mountains is dangerous and destructive, twelve-year-
old Reba Castillo decides to try to save it from the bounty hunter
seeking to kill it.
    ISBN 0-310-54351-7 (paper)
    [1. Wolverines—Fiction. 2. Wildlife conservation—Fiction.
3. San Gabriel Mountains (Calif.)—Fiction. 4. California—Fiction.
5. Mexican Americans—Fiction.] I. Title.
PZ7.B7388Bo   1992
[Fic]—dc20   92–7713
                                                                CIP
                                                                AC

All rights reserved. No part of this publication may be reproduced, stored in
a retrieval system, or transmitted in any form or by any means—electronic,
mechanical, photocopy, recording, or any other—except for brief quotations
in printed reviews, without the prior permission of the publisher.

Edited by Dave Lambert
Interior designed by Louise Bauer
Cover designed by Gary Gnidovic
Cover illustration by Matthew Archambault

Printed in the United States of America

93 94 95 96 97 / DH / 10 9 8 7 6 5 4 3 2

Dedicated with much love
to the Castillo family:
Bob, Fay, Luke, Andy, Beckita, Timmy

Contents

Contents

*"If we are to love wild animals so much
that we do not want to kill them
we must know them as they actually live."*
—James Oliver Curwood, author of Baree,
the Story of a Wolf-Dog *and* The Bear
(also a major motion picture)

*"The wind blows where it wishes and you hear
the sound of it, but do not know where it comes from
and where it is going; so is everyone who is born
of the Spirit."*
—Jesus, in John 3:8

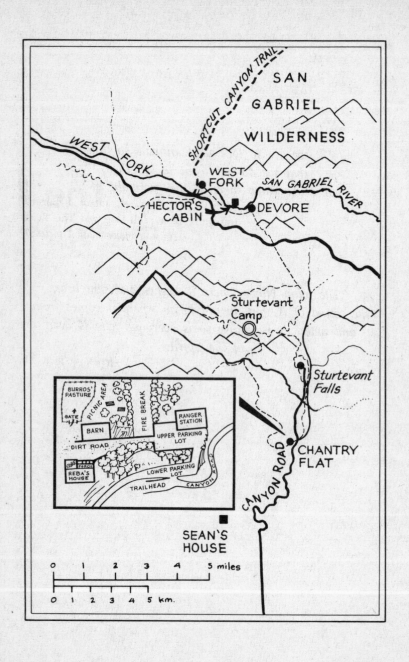

SAN GABRIEL WILDERNESS

SHORTCUT CANYON TRAIL

WEST FORK

WEST FORK

SAN GABRIEL RIVER

HECTOR'S CABIN

DEVORE

Sturtevant Camp

Sturtevant Falls

BURROS' PASTURE

PICNIC AREA

FIRE BREAK

GATE

BARN

RANGER STATION

UPPER PARKING LOT

DIRT ROAD

REBA'S HOUSE

LOWER PARKING LOT

TRAILHEAD

CANYON

CANYON ROAD

CHANTRY FLAT

SEAN'S HOUSE

0   1   2   3   4   5 miles

0   1   2   3   4   5 km.

1
The
Primeval
Thing

I was supposed to be taking in the laundry, but instead I
lay in a clearing, comfortably on my back, cushioned by
dusty pine needles just above our Chantry Flat pack station.
I kept telling Mama she needed to get a dryer. But noooo.
She always said the wind was the best dryer around. Our
clothes, all four of us kids' and Mama's, flapped on the top
of the hill, like white wings.

A heavy, hot silence hung in the small clearing. The dry
heat pressed on me all the way through. Down below, past
the burros' corral where the small park, ranger station, and
our pack station were, the Santa Ana winds fought. The

fierce winds hadn't bullied their way into the clearing. I was glad. After three days of Santa Ana winds, devil winds as they were sometimes called, I was tired of wrestling with them.

At the curved edge of the clearing, my baby burro Burrito stood, one hind leg cocked, his eyes closed and his bottle-brush tail swishing his flanks like a windshield wiper. He was truly my baby. His dam died after he was foaled. She had hemorrhaged so fast that she bled to death before we could even call the veterinarian. So I took care of him, bottle-feeding him at all kinds of weird hours. He hated when I went to school and would bray after me.

I sighed happily and looked up. The sky had hardened into an unending stretch of blue. A fighter jet, probably an F-16 from Edwards Air Force Base, went overhead, its engine screaming seconds after it passed over. One of my uncles, Bob Castillo, was in the Air Force (not Edwards—he was stationed in New Jersey) and he would tell me about the different jets he worked on. Not the top secret ones though.

I sat up. Speaking of top secret. My mom didn't know where I was. She had told me to get the laundry almost two hours ago. I had run off without answering. I could almost hear her: "Reba, I don't like you walking alone in the mountains."

Me: "Mama! I grew up in these mountains. I know them better than I know myself."

Mama giving me her famous furious suppressed look. "I mean it, Reba. Not alone."

"I have Burrito with me."

"A burro is not a human."

Gee, I didn't know that. But I didn't dare say that out loud. Even though I'd be thirteen in exactly two months and three days, she'd smack me for being smart for a comment like that.

When I *was* alone in the mountains, against Mama's wishes, I made myself feel less guilty by staying on well-marked trails. That seemed a good compromise. I would leave Mama a note telling her the basic direction I was going, too, in case a mutant bear got me. That way they'd find my body.

I chuckled and sat up. Time to get the laundry and go home before it got later. I stood. The pine needles crunched under my tennis shoes.

Cream-colored Burrito, just shy of seven months, was nosing the dusty ground, tail still swinging, sometimes catching on a brambly bush, popping twigs when he'd yank it free. "Let's go, Burrito."

But instead of walking leisurely out with me, Burrito stiffened, his head thrust up like a periscope and his long pale ears shot forward. Dribbles of sunlight blended him into the shadows and light.

What was he looking at? I studied the clearing. Cropped grass, courtesy of Burrito, and hunched oak trees, dusty filthy from the lack of rain, stood quietly in and around the clearing. Chunks of white-veined granite stuck out between the trees like broken teeth.

Burrito faced the edge of the clearing where Mama's laundry flapped between two sturdy knobcone pines. Next to the burro was a stand of ten-foot trees, their tops bowing in the heavier winds.

What did he sense? Coyote? Burros hate coyotes. They'll chase them. And lately the coyotes had been bolder than ever because of the drought. To get food and water, the wild animals had to come around people. Sean, my best friend, had seen his neighbor's cat killed by a couple of coyotes early one morning. The two coyotes, brown lines, had swooped down on the grey tabby and broken her back with one bite. Sean had watched them tear the cat apart.

When I asked why he hadn't opened his window and yelled, he had said quietly that seeing the coyotes had made him want to hide; he had feared getting their attention even though he was safe in the house.

"It was a primeval thing," he had told me. His mom is a psychologist, which explains the weird things he says sometimes.

But in the clearing, Burrito was still at attention, long ears straight up, his nostrils wide circles.

Sometimes the burros saw phantoms. Uncle Hector, who lives up by West Fork and isn't really my uncle but might as well be, says animals can see through the walls of heaven and hell. "*Sí*, burros, they bray when they see the devil," Uncle Hector will insist, his round face serious, but his eyes laugh. Well, maybe.

I crossed the clearing and stood only a few feet from the flapping laundry. The wicker basket for clean clothes sat on a tan patch of dirt, empty except for a couple of baby pinecones that had fallen in, shaken by the hot winds. Burrito jumped when I touched his shoulder. Then I tugged at his choppy, milky white mane.

"Let's go," I said. The winds shifted, swirling, a whirlwind, and the most awful rank scent surrounded us.

Burrito gave a frightened gasp and sprang sideways into me, knocking me on my butt. Burrito leaped clear over me, his tail an exclamation point, and galloped out of the clearing, down the hill, heading for home.

I yelled for him to whoa—just as a branch popped in the knobcone tree shadows.

"Who's there?" My voice quavered like a high-tension wire in the Santa Ana devil winds.

No one answered. Another branch popped, up in the knobcone, higher than me. The rank scent increased. What in the world was that stink? Worse than the septic tank leaking.

Warily I rose and walked to the tree. Its trunk was as big around as a burro's girth. The clothesline circled it once, tied in a tidy bowline knot by my oldest brother, Pio.

"Who's there?" I asked again, louder this time. Burrito gave a sharp half bray in the distance: his warning cry. Then another bray followed: his baby cry. Come and save me! I'm only a helpless burro.

A branch popped a third time, the sound lower this time. I looked up. Something, a bulky animal, as big as a grown burro's head, hunched above me in the shadowy light.

A skunk? They don't climb trees. Possum? Too big for a possum and they smell, but not that bad—I know because I'd raised a couple of orphans. A mountain lion cub? Except they're tawny, not dark.

The animal's eyes shone in a ray of sunlight hitting him across the face. He looked straight at me, deliberately lifting a wide front paw and stepping down on a dry branch. The branch cracked. The animal stared into my eyes, like he was trying to get my attention.

No, that was loco, crazy.

I wanted to snatch up a rock or stick to fling at him, but the closest was a large, flat rock off beside another tree. I took one step back to get it when Burrito let loose his baby cry once more, ending on a frantic note.

The animal had something white in his mouth. My heart pounded—a cat? Maury, the park ranger, had Mango, an orange-striped queen. Cat or not, this whatever-it-was-animal was killing too near the campground.

Suddenly, the animal launched out of the tree like a kid jumping from a swing. If I'd been the screaming type I would have split air molecules. Instead, I threw my arms over my head and ducked. He brushed me, his fur tickling my bare arms. That awful smell!

I looked up, feeling like a wimp. Ducking from an animal.

The beast stood under the waving laundry in the full blaze of the sunlight. The white thing in his mouth wasn't an animal. I clapped my hand over my mouth. It was a pair of Mama's underwear!

The animal twisted away, bounded along the granite-studded ridge, and dropped down on the opposite side of the park. Slatey rocks rattled, then quiet.

I ran to the top of the ridge, stood on a freckled boulder, and looked across the mountainside.

Nothing. It was gone, just like that. I shaded my eyes. Cholla cactus cities covered the hillside, broken rocks filling in between them like a mosaic pattern. The bad smell was fading.

I walked back to the laundry. Slowly the clearing began to fill again with the sound of birds' songs. I hadn't even realized the birds had stopped until now. They had been afraid.

Burrito called me again, closer now.

I waded through a patch of manzanita bushes and greasewood, my arms over my head to avoid getting scratched, and came to the main trail up the ridge. Burrito rushed up and pressed his nose under my arm. I hugged his thin neck, wondering about the strange animal—and wondering how to explain to Mama that it had stolen a pair of her underwear. The animal was nothing I'd seen before in these mountains. I had thought I knew everything about the mountains, but I didn't know so much after all.

2

Darkest Before Dawn

That night I lay on my stomach—my younger brother, Andres, says like a warthog, as if he knows how a warthog sleeps—and I dreamed.

In my dream, the heat from the autumn Santa Ana winds burned over our house, seeping through the screens and into the open windows. I tossed restlessly. In my room, Burrito snorted and tossed his head nervously, his long ears flickering. What was he doing in the house? I've never let him in before. Mama would kill us both.

This is a dream, Reba, I sternly told myself.

But it seems real, I thought, and slid deeper into it.

Burrito gave another snort, then a loud, long burro bray tore through the night. I sat up. Alarmingly awake. I was on my feet, untwisting my oversized tee-shirt nightgown as I ran down the tiny hallway. I unlocked the screen door in one quick move, leaped onto the front porch, and sprang down the steps, my bare feet stinging in the dirt, but running.

Mama's voice called behind me, brittle and sharp as dried thistles: "Reba! Reba! Where are you going?"

I didn't answer because I was running so hard. All I knew was that I had to get to the barn. Overhead the hot winds snarled through the stand of white oaks around the pack station, whipping their branches into a mad dance. Other burros' cries mingled with Burrito's.

I plunged into the dark barn and hit the lights. Instantly, the shining pools of light chased back some of the burros' heated fear. All twelve burros were wide-eyed, their heads over the low stall doors, staring at me.

"What's happening, you guys?" I asked them and walked down the uneven cement aisle, touching a soft muzzle in a stall on one side, stroking a long ear on the other side. I looked in on Burrito, so small in the large stall.

But he wasn't alone.

Burrito sprang against the stall door when he saw me, sobbing in brays. I threw open the latch. He poured out and knocked me down for the second time in twenty-four hours. I hit the hard cement floor.

His strange companion shot out past me, a stream of dark with broad lines of cream color along his back and sides, jetting low to the ground, snarling. As it passed by, like the afterburn of a jet, that familiar and unpleasant rank smell filled my nostrils. It leaped to the top of a stall divider next to an empty stall, crossed it as nimbly as a tightrope walker, and sprang through an open window.

What was it? I shuddered, remembering how he'd looked me so boldly in my eye.

Mama appeared in the door, her hair down, long and

18

curling over her shoulders. Her cotton nightgown rippled as she approached. She untangled me from under Burrito's legs and helped me up. My little burro trotted down the aisle to Mozo, his sire, and they stood touching noses. Burrito gasped out his fear and Mozo licked Burrito's face with his big tongue.

Pio, my oldest brother, appeared and stood over me, bare legs thick like tree stumps, his hands on his hips and his dark eyes wide awake. "What's going on, Reba?" he asked calmly.

All the burros still stared, their sepia-colored eyes rolling. They cast worried glances over their furry shoulders.

Pio sniffed. "What's that awful smell?"

I turned to Mama to explain that I'd smelled the same smell this afternoon when *he* came through the door.

He was Francisco, Mama's boyfriend. Or as my friend, Sean, says, "Your mom's *boyfiend*."

"What's he doing here?" I demanded. It's not like he was visiting late. It was, like, three in the morning.

Mama's voice tightened like a sash. "Reba," she said, warningly, her voice rising. "Is this some kind of joke? Because if it is—"

"It's not!" I said. "Something was bothering the burros. Didn't you hear them? They woke me up." I told her about the animal up in the trees. But not about the underwear. I was afraid she wouldn't believe me.

I finished with, "I didn't tell you when I got home because you and Francisco were busy." I choked over his name, then glanced at him in gym shorts, bare chested. Like he belonged here.

Miguel, my second-oldest brother, peered in the barn from the door, rubbing his eyes. "What's going on?" he asked. Only Andres, my little brother, was missing. Great. One of the few times we all got together and it had to be here at three in the morning.

"Reba's chasing imaginary things," said Pio.

"I am not!" I clenched my fists, trying to visualize the animal from this afternoon so I could describe it. It was the same animal—it had to be—that had been with Burrito just now.

Francisco walked down the aisle. He hadn't been in much of a hurry to see what was going on; he'd put on tennis shoes and even tied them. Mama was barefoot; so were my brothers.

"Explain, Reba," said Mama.

"Some animal was in Burrito's stall," I said.

Francisco looked in the stall.

"Not now," I said, disgusted. "It ran off. I think it was a dog or something." I knew it wasn't a dog, so why was I lying?

"A dog," Mama repeated. We had no dogs up here, except dogs brought by hikers.

"Maybe a coyote?" offered Pio.

Mama frowned. "I heard rabies was going around again. Maybe we better vaccinate the burros." She sighed. "So expensive though."

Pio yawned. "It was probably just a restless coyote," he said. "Anyway, I got a test tomorrow. I'm going back to bed." Pio went to Pasadena City College, PCC. Sean and I called it Pasadena Child Care.

"Look, Mama," said Miguel, suddenly. He was bent over Burrito. "There are some scratches on him."

I rushed over to my little burro and studied his white, fuzzy shoulder. A line of fur on his shoulder looked like a snag in a nylon. Blood had welled up. Mama shrugged.

"He could have gotten those anywhere," she said with a shrug. "Reba takes him all over kingdom come."

"But those are fresh," I said. I went to the tack room and opened the medicine box. I doctored the cuts with the yellow powder.

Burrito still trembled when I was done so I opened

Mozo's stall door and let him in. The two fell together, gasping and nuzzling.

"Reba," said Mama. "You spoil that animal."

But Burrito needed his papa tonight. Whatever had been in his stall hadn't been paying a friendly visit. Had the animal also been after Burrito this afternoon? I shivered.

Mama was staring at me. "Back to bed," she said. Francisco poked around the feed room. As if the animal would stay around here. It was probably halfway to Winter Creek by now.

"You don't believe me, do you?" I asked her.

"Reba," she said, brushing her hair back, "no accusations, okay? It's late. Or early, or something. Let's just go back to bed. We'll talk in the morning."

What if the animal came back? I straightened up. "I'm staying out here."

Mama shook her head. "Reba," she started, but Miguel interrupted her.

"I'll stay with her, Mama," he said. "I think she's right. Something was after the burros. It probably won't come back, but just in case."

Mama looked very tired. A pang of sorrow struck me. I really didn't mean to upset her—

"Okay, Miguel," Mama said, and took Francisco's hand.

Miguel made a gagging face and pointed to Francisco as they walked back to the house. Miguel didn't like Francisco because he made him do lots of chores. But I had a different reason. Like he wasn't my father.

After checking in each stall once more, Miguel ran back to the house for a couple of blankets and our pillows. When he came back, I snuggled down in the stall with Burrito and Mozo. Miguel went into the aisle, spread some fresh bedding straw, and lay down. We turned off the interior lights, but left the outside light burning. The boards creaked in the

21

wind, but the old barn was strong. One stream of air made Burrito's tail ripple.

"What did you really see?" Miguel asked from the aisle.

"I don't know." A piece of straw poked my elbow. I wriggled around, straw stirring.

Miguel laughed. "I thought you were the mountain goddess here. Knowing all the animals." He said it in a teasing voice, but it was underlined with seriousness.

"Not this animal," I said after a moment.

We were quiet and I thought he'd fallen asleep when he said, "Don't get so upset about Francisco. It's not worth it."

I wasn't sure what he meant by "it," but I appreciated the kindness in his voice.

Finally I relaxed with Burrito curled up at my feet and Mozo standing watch over us. I turned over and opened my eyes a moment. Something white was under the manger. I raised myself on my elbow and looked closer. Mama's underwear from this afternoon.

I swallowed a laugh—and then a frightening thought hit me. The animal had been in powerful Mozo's stall, too!

I sat up, my heart pounding, as if the animal was right there focusing his intense stare on me. Miguel had gone to sleep, his breathing loud and slow. I took the underwear and stuffed it under my blankets.

No wonder people feared the unknown. That was the scariest thing of all.

"I'll protect you, Burrito," I whispered, and hoped I could. The baby burro twitched his ears and slept on.

3
The Great
White
Hunter

Four hours later, I was scooping up burro poop with the pitchfork and dumping it into the wheelbarrow. I was glad to see, when I wheeled the manure out to the compost pile, that Francisco's car was gone.

I stabbed the pitchfork into the manure and straw, emptied the wheelbarrow, and rolled it back into the barn for another load.

Andres, my little brother, who'd slept through all of the-animal-in-the-barn-no-it's-only-Reba-going-loco, worked on the other aisle. He was ten, three years younger than me. When he was born I thought he was a toy. Mama found me playing with him early one morning. I'd taken him from his crib and carried him outside to a fort I'd built out of rocks. Andres had lain gurgling on his belly, surrounded by Miguel's discarded army men.

I only remember Mama's scream when she found him missing. Then she had run outside and seen us. She had laughed and laughed until she cried. Which I had found very odd, laughing and crying at the same time. When I cried I wasn't in the mood to laugh.

I paused, looking out one of the tiny windows. Sunlight burned down like liquid glass. The devil winds snarled off the Mojave, bringing with them the desert heat to our mountains and down to the cities around Los Angeles. I couldn't blame the desert for wanting to get rid of it.

I stabbed at a great pile of manure, wondering how a small burro could poop so much, when Sean yelled my name from the porch.

"There's your boyfriend," said Andres with a toss of manure at me. It splatted on the cement floor. Automatically part of my brain thought, *One of the burros has loose stools. Better mention it to Mama.*

Andres tossed another forkful at me. The other part of my brain thought, *Attack.* I threw a shovelful back at him.

"Shut up," I said savagely. Sean was not my boyfriend. "You have poop for brains," I told Andres. Sean called again and Andres just laughed in that snarky way he had.

I ran to the entrance of the barn. "Here," I yelled, glad to see Sean. He wasn't my boyfriend, but my best friend.

Sean jumped down off our big wide front porch. The country store we ran on weekends and summers took up most of the porch.

"How did you get here so early?" I asked as he crossed the dust to the barn. Sometimes if he got lucky, his older sister or brother would drive him the four miles up here, or on very rare occasions even his mom, who didn't like me much, although Sean protested that she did. Mostly he either biked up, which took a good couple hours—the road was awesomely steep—or walked the shortcut through the hills, which took about forty-five minutes—also steep.

A couple of our red-and-brown chickens peeled away from him as he ran over, grinning. His blonde hair shone in the hot light. "Bryan drove me," he said. Bryan, his older brother, worked at the Santa Anita Race Track as a track handicapper. I'd been begging Bryan to take us for the day. I loved all horses, but especially the thin, beautiful thorough-breds. But Bryan wouldn't. He always said that he was working, not babysitting.

"Well, that was pretty nice of him," I said.

"I bribed him," said Sean, and we walked back inside the barn, still cool compared with the hot, furious morning. "I gave him five dollars."

I stopped. Sean was saving for a new mountain bike, with eighteen gears. "You shouldn't have," I said.

He just grinned and grabbed another pitchfork. "Don't worry," he said. "When Bryan was in the shower I took the five bucks out of his wallet."

We burst out laughing. Sean helped Andres and me finish mucking out the barn. Andres never said anything to Sean's face about being my boyfriend. Sean gave him comic books to read, so Andres didn't want to kill a good thing.

After cleaning, I was free for the rest of the day. Tomorrow, Sunday, I'd have to take my turn in the country store. But tomorrow was a thousand years away.

"Let's go down in the canyon. It'll be cooler," I said. The water in the canyon stream was cold.

On our way out, I stepped into the stall where the beast had leaped through the window; I peered outside. "No footprints there," I said. The winds could have blown them away, it was so dry. No mud for the mysterious creature to step in.

"Footprints?" Sean walked over, a line of sunlight gleaming off his glasses.

I told him. About seeing the animal in the tree. How it stole Mama's underwear—he didn't even laugh at that, he could tell how serious it was. Then about the beast in Burrito's stall and how it left the underwear and ran off.

I didn't tell him about Francisco being here last night, all night. I didn't know if he'd understand how I felt about it, his parents being together and all. Besides, I was embarrassed.

Sean frowned and sat next to me on a bale of hay. The wind coming through the small barn windows made his hair stand up like it was punked.

"Now that I think about it," I said, "I don't think the animal hurt Burrito."

He pushed his glasses up higher on his nose. "How do you figure?"

"Because Burrito would have been even more hysterical. Remember when he cut his hind foot?"

Sean rolled his eyes. "I'll say. He was a wimpy burro that day."

Burrito had moaned and groaned all the way home. Mostly he'd been mad because I wouldn't share my lunch with him. Burrito had a passion for Mama's tortillas. I'm not very generous.

Sean had gotten up and was prowling around the barn. "Tell me again, exactly what happened," he said. "In the barn, I mean."

I described the whole deal to him again while I pulled bridles down off the pegs for Chihuahua and Vinegar. Mama let us ride them because they were very old burros, more than thirty years old. Mama figured they were smart enough to keep us out of trouble. Sean poked around Burrito's stall while I waited, the bridles slung on my shoulder.

Sean and I had been friends since third grade, when I had defended him against this bully of a fifth grader who had decided he wanted to pound Sean into the ground and make *pazole* stew out of him.

I surprised the fifth grader by jumping on him from behind and riding him like a mad cat on a dog. After staggering around the four-square outlines, he collapsed under my weight. I was also kicking him in the ribs, which helped. To finish him off, I bit his shoulder. Hard. He bled a lot and they took him to emergency. He didn't taste too good, either. I almost got suspended from school, but the bully had a history, so they believed me when I said it was self-defense. And it was—almost.

From then on, Sean and I were friends.

"Look," Sean said from inside the stall. On some splinters of worn, grey board was a clump of black hairs. Coarse black hair. Burrito was pale as moonlight.

"How long has Burrito been in this stall?" asked Sean.

"Always," I said. "This was Rosa's stall—his mother."

"What color was she?" asked Sean. "I can't keep them all straight."

I chewed on a strand of my hair, remembering Rosa. She would sit down if she thought you packed her too heavy. "She was a chestnut," I said.

Sean held out the fur. It didn't feel at all like burro fur. I wasn't sure how I knew the difference, just that I knew the feel of burro fur after brushing them for years. This fur belonged to something else.

Sean put the fur to his nose and fell back into the straw. "Yuck," he said. He handed it to me and I sniffed it. Bad stuff.

"That's the smell from this morning," I said. "And from yesterday afternoon."

"Skunk?" asked Sean.

Then we both shook our heads. Skunks get hit on the road all the time and we knew their acrid smell all too well.

"Coyote?" asked Sean, stuffing the hairs in his jeans pocket.

I shook my head again. "It wasn't tall enough. Unless it

was a baby coyote. But it's the wrong time of year for baby coyotes. Not to mention wrong color."

"Platypus? Tasmanian devil? Hoary bat?" he asked. I gave him my best you-are-so-weird look.

He unlatched the gate and we walked up the steep hill towards the burros, the reins swinging at my side.

"Ring-tailed lemur? Capybara? Tyrannosaurus rex?" he went on.

He thought he knew so much. I kicked at him. "For that, you get Chihuahua."

"Aw, not Chihuahua." But he was laughing.

Chihuahua was just that. Tiny. But he was strong. You just looked like an idiot riding him.

"It's your turn anyway," I told him. "I rode him last time." We bridled the burros and led them out. We jumped aboard and headed out of the park with Burrito following like an overgrown puppy.

We rode down the hill, through the steep picnic area with its many tables and benches. Some days every table was filled with kids and grown-ups. A lot of birthday parties happened up here. A couple of times Sean and I dressed a burro in a clown outfit and the kids loved it. No one offered to pay us though. We had hoped to make some bucks.

Burrito stuck his head in a trash can and I had to whack his skinny rump before he would move on.

The ranger station where Maury Aaseng lived was perched on the other side of the ridge above the main canyon leading to Sturtevant Falls, Spruce Grove, Mount Wilson and, of course, Uncle Hector's place. I squinted and looked into the screened windows, wondering whether Maury was there, when a tall white man came out of the office, talking loud as if Maury were deaf.

The man's back was to us; he faced Maury, who was frowning. The man held a rifle. Sean and I looked at each other in surprise. In this high wind, and with everything so dry, no hunting or fires were allowed. Extreme fire danger—everyone knew that.

Burrito sauntered up behind the man. The tips of Burrito's white ears were only as tall as the man's waist. The baby burro stood, head cocked, then he gave a huge bray right at the man's back.

Sean and I clapped our hands over our mouths, laughing madly.

The man whirled. His eyes were like blue flames.

He shoved Burrito aside with his foot, like my burro was a dead stump. "Hey, you kids," he said. "Come here."

4

Keepers of the Mountains

Sean and I glanced at each other. If Burrito hadn't been standing near the man, we'd have ignored him and trotted the burros out of there.

"Hold Vinegar," I hissed to Sean. I jumped off, flipped the reins over her head and handed them to Sean. Walking to Burrito, I could smell stale cigarette smoke on the white man. Quickly I put my hand under Burrito's chin, pretending I had an invisible halter and lead rope on him. Burrito stepped with me. He was good at imaginary games.

The white man slung his rifle against his broad shoulder and asked, "Where do you kids ride around here?"

I pretended I didn't know English. That usually works, since so many Hispanics in Southern California speak only Spanish—although having Sean with me probably blew my cover. I didn't know why I wanted to get away from this man, but I did—I really did. I hurried Burrito back to Vinegar. Sean handed me the reins. I swung on her bony back and kicked her ribs.

The burros jogged along the curve of the asphalt road toward the trailhead with Burrito tucked between Vinegar and Chihuahua. A three-quarter-ton black Dodge pick-up was parked off to the side, under a few scraggly digger pines. The man called after us again, but we didn't answer.

As we rode past the truck, two red Doberman pinschers leaped up from the truck bed, startling all of us. They barked deep and black, reminding me of a story I'd read about a three-headed dog guarding the gates of hell. The dogs stretched over the curved metal side of the truck, yellow-eyed, lips wrinkled back showing dagger teeth.

Our burros shied, then whirled to face the dogs. Burrito still was tucked between the adult burros.

"Quiet down!" roared the man. Both dogs dropped like he'd shot them. Chains clunked. What if the dogs hadn't been chained?

Burros fight to the death—at least that's what all the old muleskinners said. Suddenly I had a strange thought: My Burrito could have been shredded, like the beef in an edible burrito. And I wasn't thinking of the dogs; but whatever animal I'd seen yesterday could have killed him, if it had wanted to. Deep down I shivered, because I knew I couldn't have prevented it—and last night the grown burros had been caught in their stalls, so they couldn't have prevented it either.

Now there was this man. And suddenly I knew: This white man had something to do with that weird animal.

I tried to urge Vinegar down the road, but she didn't want to put her back to the dogs. The man marched up to us.

He was tall—over six feet, I'll bet—and big, but not fat. He tried to smile, which looked scarier than his anger.

"Hey, kids, nice burros," he said. His voice was hoarse, like he had a chest cold.

Burrito stared at him with his amber-colored eyes, fascinated. I planted my foot in his little chest to be sure he didn't saunter over again.

"Thanks," said Sean, finally. His feet hung almost to the ground from little scruffy Chihuahua. If he pointed his toes, they would touch.

"I just want to ask you kids a couple of questions," he said. "Friends, okay?"

I'd rather be friends with a rattlesnake. Sean and I exchanged glances. We didn't have much choice at the moment. It wouldn't be too difficult for him to figure out where the burros and I lived. And if he complained to Mama, she'd be after me big time.

"What kind of questions?" I finally said.

He turned his fierce blue gaze on me. "So, the little *muchacha* can speak."

I gave him a withering glare. "Don't you know there's no hunting because the mountains are so dry?" I added, ever the keeper of the San Gabriels. When Sean and I were in third grade, we had discovered one of our great tasks in life: We were keepers of the San Gabriel Mountains.

"Who are you?" Sean asked.

The man opened his truck door and carefully hung his rifle over the rear window. The dogs poked their heads back up and one began growling. "Down," he bellowed. Both dogs dropped out of sight. He stepped back toward us, leaving the cab door open, and announced, "I'm a bounty hunter." He might as well have said, "Normal rules don't apply to me."

"Hunting what?" I asked. I had thought bounty hunters were things of the past, like in old Westerns.

The man raised his right eyebrow and showed his teeth

33

again in what he must have thought was a smile. I think I looked like that when the dentist worked on my teeth.

"Right now that's classified information," he said. "I want to know if you two ride a lot in the mountains."

We nodded unhappily to his question.

"I want you to keep a sharp lookout for anything unusual," he said.

I thought of that weird beast.

"Do you mean people?" asked Sean. "Like jailbreakers, or something?" I knew Sean was thinking of the animal, too.

The man lit a cigarette, took a drag, and said into the bluish smoke, "I'm not saying right now. Just keep your eyes peeled, okay? Call me if you see anything strange." He handed us each a shiny white business card with his name, "Kane Marshall," in raised letters, an address in Sierra Madre, and a couple of phone numbers. That's all. Nothing after his name or anything explaining who he was. Not even bounty hunter.

"Don't you know there's no smoking?" I said. "Extreme fire danger." Normally Maury would practically hose down a smoker.

Mr. Marshall swung into his truck, settling on the black bench seat, not answering. He slammed the door shut. His dogs popped back up like jacks-in-the-box and bared their teeth in silent snarls. He started the motor and called out the window, "There might be some nice reward money, too."

Oh, yeah, as if he could buy us off.

The truck roared off, spewing exhaust and dust. Burrito coughed loudly. Sean tore up the business card and threw it to the wind.

"Five-hundred-dollar fine for littering," I said. But it wasn't funny.

Sean curled his lip. "What a first-class jerk."

I tucked the card in my pants pocket. Just in case. You never knew when you might need something.

"Let's go talk to Maury," I said. We rode back to the

34

ranger station. Burrito pushed his nose against the screen door and gave a half-bray, like a sobbing gasp.

Maury came to the door. "Hey, y'all," he said. He has this funny accent because he's from Texas. His hair's bright red and he has freckles all over his face, and his arms and back, too. Once he let Andres connect the freckles on his back with a pen, like playing a dot-to-dot.

"Who was that guy?" asked Sean.

Maury shook his head mournfully, like a horse with colic. "He's kind of, what's the word, abrasive, ain't he?"

"He's like mega-jalapeños," Sean said.

"He's like falling on a cholla cactus," I said.

"You don't have to tell me," said Maury. "He comes in here showing me this fancy license, saying he can hunt any exotic animal in these mountains."

"Animal," I said.

"Not a person," said Sean. But we'd known that already.

I wondered: What *was* that in the stall with Burrito that would attract a bounty hunter?

"Animal," said Maury. "I pity it, though, whatever beastie it might be."

"Did he say?" I asked.

Maury shook his head. "Hush-hush for some reason."

"But, Maury," I said, "you're the ranger here. You're in charge."

He raised his ruddy eyebrows. "Nope. That guy's got rank on me. Foolish if you ask me," Maury went on. " 'That animal dangerous?' I asked him and he won't say another word. 'I got hikers and packers to think of,' I tell him. But he don't care."

That's grown-ups for you. I rolled my eyes. They are worse than kids sometimes.

"What's going to happen?" I asked.

Maury shrugged. "He'll hunt and I'll look the other way."

"Great, so what if we get shot?" said Sean, pushing up his glasses.

"Somehow I think when that man aims, he'll get what he wants and it's not you," said Maury.

"No one wants you, Sean," I said. He stuck out his tongue at me.

Maury waved us off. "Don't you worry. You got your burros with you. They'll keep you safe."

I wasn't so sure about that anymore.

Sean and I finally started down the Gabrielino trail into the canyon. The winds were quieter there. We spent the rest of the day wading in the East Fork River—water only to our knees, but bone-chilling cold—and hunting for gold. Abandoned silver and gold mines dotted the mountains, and we always hoped for a vein. I almost forgot about the animal and the man who hunted it. Almost, but not quite.

5
Early Morning Surprise

Sunday mornings, no one in my family got up early—except me. Our country store didn't open until eleven. Before six A.M., I turned the burros out into the pasture and tossed them some hay flakes. They sunbathed and crunched breakfast. Afterwards, Burrito drowsed in the light slanting through the sugar pines, a flash of white among the darker trees and shadows.

When they seemed content, I got my backpack and hiked above their pasture to the bare ridge behind Chantry Flat. A slide of dirt unfurled, disappearing dustily into a thicket of yellowish yarrow, crowns of chamise, and strong-branched manzanita bushes. I smiled, wishing I was small enough to explore that elfin forest of stunted bushes—like bonsai almost, yet thick with wildness.

The park, with its steep picnic grounds, was on the pasture side of the ridge, but from where I was the park was hidden by a stand of maul oaks—not tall, but curved and gnarled. Back down the road from the park, past the steep, small canyon, was where the cities poured out to Los Angeles: Sierra Madre, the rustic canyon town where Sean lived. Pasadena, old and earthquake-shaky. Rich Arcadia, where Thoroughbred horses lived as kings. The whole of the San Gabriel valley opened up, flattened like a penny run over by a train, all the way to the Pacific Ocean. Today, as usual, the valley was hazy from blowing dust and smog.

Some days when the sky had been scoured clean by wind or rain, I saw Catalina Island. "No way," Sean would tell me. "It's a hundred miles from here." But I had seen it, floating in veils of fog. I figured Sean was just jealous because he wore glasses while I could see nearly as well as a hawk.

The winds sputtered along in hot gusts. On top of the ridge, I sat on a big outcropping of granite and tucked my feet up, facing east where piles of mountains lay.

Old Baldy was the tallest mountain in the San Gabriels, at over 10,000 feet. In fourth grade I went skiing there with Sean and his parents. Exciting, but scary. Papa had taught me to snowshoe when I was about five, the slow tramp over the snow. More humble, but in a way I liked it better. Even though I haven't snowshoed since.

A little snow still clung to the peak of Old Baldy, probably left over from two or more years ago. It hadn't rained in so long. I thought backwards and remembered rain on my face when I was in second grade; now I was in sixth.

As always, I added the lack of rain to my prayers.

Each Sunday I said pretty much the same thing: "Oh God, please let my father come back home. Make my brothers stop picking on me. And if you don't want any of this to happen, and if I get mad about it, forgive me, okay?"

Then there was the animal in Burrito's stall. I wasn't sure what to say about that. So I sat staring at Old Baldy like I was hypnotized.

Papa used to say he was part Indian, the old Gabrielino tribe from right here in these mountains. So that makes me part that, too. Mama says Papa is loco, that no California Indians have survived. But I like to think that maybe in my veins, and Papa's too, we carry a small part of the Gabrielino's peaceful ways.

Papa told me that the Gabrielino Indians believe creation happened on Old Baldy. So I figured it was good to pray facing its peak, just in case. Besides, it is the king of the San Gabriels.

I scratched my nose. It was peeling again. I pulled out my Bible from my backpack. I always read it on Sundays. Aunt Kate, really Mama's niece, had given it to me the Christmas after Papa left us, in the days when rain still fell.

I'd already read all the verses about horses and burros. Now I was working on reading the stories about Jesus. I wished more of the stories were about when he was a kid, but the grown-up stories were okay. Mama told me once that the stories in the Bible weren't true, that they were just that: stories. But I'd rather think that they're real; I like the idea of Balaam's donkey really talking to him. I wished Burrito would talk to me. Maybe someday. After all, Balaam was grown up when his donkey talked.

I read for a while, stopped, looked at the mountains, and read some more.

Down below, cars were beginning to growl into the parking lot. I stood, stretched, and put away the Bible. Then I shouldered my pack and started back along the ridge. A couple of Stellar's jays, blue-black and beautiful, squawked and soared off, their tailfeathers spread like fingers.

Just before I started down the ridge, I passed through a

dense family of knobcone pines, pushing aside their boughs with the tiny, hard cones that open only in forest fires. A familiar rank scent stopped me.

I carefully studied the ground between the trees around me, splashed with sunlight, but didn't see the animal. Maybe it had just passed through. I leaned against a thick knobcone, the rough bark scratching through my shirt. The rest of the ridge seemed quiet. Maybe the animal lived in a burrow. I looked for an opening in the ground, but saw only small snake holes.

The scent was getting stronger, making my eyes water, like they did when I have to clean house using ammonia. But I still didn't see the animal.

Then I knew.

My fingers turned cold and my stomach clenched like it does before I throw up. Slowly I backed away from the big pine tree. I looked up into its dense boughs.

Two eyes stared down at me.

6

The
Robot
Factor

I froze, so still that each heartbeat gently pushed my body in tiny jerks. My blood rushed in my ears. My breath, when I couldn't hold it any longer, sounded like an ocean rushing to the shore.

The animal stared down at me, his eyes yellow with black cat slits. His body was the size of a cocker spaniel. The shadows of the branches wavered in the slight breeze. I let my breath out slowly like a tire wheezing and took another deep breath. That rank smell. Probably how a Tyrannosaurus rex would smell.

"Who are you?" I asked, softly.

At my voice the animal stepped down onto a lower limb. Gold sunlight flecked across his dark spine and shone on the pale cream bands of color lengthwise around its back and face, and for a moment something gleamed at his throat.

The wedge-shaped head turned towards me, sniffing, although I couldn't imagine how he could smell anything but himself. Long claws scrabbled on the branch and he climbed farther down the limb, headfirst. He paused, then leaped to the ground.

He shook himself, his coat thick and rippling, his tail well feathered. He was broad, squat, and powerful. He acted like he wasn't afraid of anything.

I believed him.

He continued gazing at me, bold. So I stared back. Scared, but not terrified. Part of me wanted to run, part wanted to stay and—and what, Reba? I didn't know.

He turned on wide paws, cool as any homeboy on his turf. Then all of a sudden I knew him. In school I'd done a report about weasels, family Mustelidae. I used to tell Andres that he was a member of the Mustelidae family, not the Castillo family.

And this animal with his smooth manners and sharp eyes was a member of the weasel family. He was a wolverine. He blinked his harvest-moon eyes as if agreeing with me.

But wolverines lived way up north, didn't they? Not in Southern California.

Our gazes locked again. "Why are you here?" I asked him. "Are you hungry? Is that why you're around?" Maury had told us that a lot of small game were dying because of the lack of water and food—grass and seeds—and that, in turn, the coyotes and mountain lions were also beginning to starve. Probably this wolverine was having a hard time, too.

He tipped his head. His were ears low and lean against his skull, but pricked forward at me, like little periscopes. The Santa Ana winds breathed through his dense fur.

"A tortilla?" I asked. "I'll bring you a tortilla from home."

I backed away, through the grasses, feeling as if I should bow or curtsy. The wolverine held his head high. Because I wasn't watching where I was going, thorns scratched my bare ankles.

His eyes gleamed after me in the morning wind. Halfway down the hill I ran for the house, flew up the porch and into the kitchen.

"Reba, *mi hija*," called Mama. She had on an apron and her hands were floured, making tortillas. Francisco sat reading the newspaper in a chair at the kitchen table. That meant he hadn't spent the night, for we received no paper; he brought one with him up the mountain when he visited. I was glad he hadn't stayed.

"Can I have a tortilla?" I asked.

Mama smiled. "Wait for breakfast."

The wolverine wouldn't wait.

"Please, Mama. I'm so starving," I said, and she gave me a level look.

Francisco smiled over the newspaper. "Reba, how goes it this morning?"

Impatience nipped me. "Okay. Just hungry." I gave Mama a pointed look.

"Gonna be a busy day at the station, no? It's a fine hiking day," he said. His mustache curved over his mouth, long and dark. With his sausage fingers, he twisted up one end, then the other.

Mama tossed me a tortilla, warm and fresh. "Don't be long. Breakfast in ten minutes."

"I won't be." I pounded back up the hill.

But the wolverine was gone.

In the trees I searched. Not there. I checked the burro pasture. The burros were still drowsing, so he wasn't there. I stood on the backbone of the ridge, city on one side, the deep mountains on the other, looking. He could be anywhere. I crouched looking for footprints. In the soft dust I found wide-toed, broad pawprints. I followed them over the ridge to the city side of the mountain; there they vanished. I sat back on my heels and sighed.

Finally I draped the tortilla over a branch where the wolverine had sat. I hoped that he, and not some other creature, would get it.

"One more prayer, *Señor Dios*," I whispered. "Will you let the wolverine get the tortilla?" God fed the sparrows, so why not the wolverines? Yet many animals were dying in the drought. Why was that?

"Who are you talking to, Reba?" asked Andres. I jumped. He appeared from behind the cluster of knobcone pines, a rock in each hand.

"What are you doing with those rocks?" I asked, suspiciously. Andres felt it was his right to heave rocks at animals, birds, and reptiles.

"For my collection," he said, innocently.

Andres did have a vast rock collection under his bed. To Mama's despair. But I didn't believe him for one minute.

"Who were you talking to?" he asked again.

"To God."

"Oh, yeah," he said. "It's Sunday."

Anyone else in my family would have thought me crazy. Maybe it was Andres's age, or maybe he thought about God, too.

"Does God talk back?" he asked, and put down the rocks, beauties, one a rose quartz, the other glitter-flecked with mica. He began to draw in the dirt with a stick.

"God doesn't talk out loud," I said. "At least not to me."

"How does he talk then?" Andres looked up at me, his own version of the stealth fighter half drawn in the dust next to the wolverine's footprint.

"I'm still figuring that out," I said. I thought he spoke in the wind, the mountains, the animals, the sky. I also thought I needed to hear more from him than that. I wanted to ask that same question to someone who heard him.

"You really think there is a God?" he asked. He drew bombs coming out of the bomber.

Guns, hunters. Yuck. I wiped my hair out of my face. "There better be a God," I said. Or I'll what? What could I do if there wasn't? Get mad at him? No one to get mad at.

"If there wasn't a God, it would be very sad, wouldn't it?" he asked.

"Very sad," I agreed.

Andres was frowning, not mad frowning. I was glad that he thought about God. It made me angry with my older brothers sometimes to think that they never seemed to think about anything they couldn't touch or see. Or eat.

"Ree-ba! An-drrr-es!"

He picked up his rocks and we walked out from under the trees. I glanced at the branch cradling the tortilla.

The tortilla was gone.

"Race you," I said. Andres and I scrambled down the hill. I let him win.

7
The Weasel Discovery

H e ate the tortilla," I told Sean on Monday afternoon in the school bus. "At least I think he ate it. It was gone from the tree."

Sean didn't answer, but kept reading a thick animal book I'd checked out from the school library. A color photo of a wolverine was on half of one page. The wolverine stared out at us with an alert expression on his small bear-like face. Sean pointed to the next page. "It says here that wolverines are in Europe, like Sweden and Russia, and over here they're in Canada and Alaska."

"But look." I'd already read over the information

47

during the fifteen minutes we get for reading each day in class. I pointed to a paragraph. "It says: 'Wolverines inhabit the Sierra Nevadas at high elevations.'"

"But those mountains are how far away? Four hundred miles, or something," asked Sean. "Does this wolverine have his own private Lear jet?" He tried to push his glasses up on his nose just as the school bus bumped; he hit himself in the face instead.

"If you want to be punched, I can do it," I said. He stuck out his tongue at me.

The last bus stop was mine. Not counting Sean who was visiting me today, only two of us got off. Andres came on an earlier bus. Miguel usually got a ride home from a friend, and Pio had his own car.

The other kid at my stop was a girl named Darcy who sometimes came over. Her parents were hippies or something. They lived in a cabin without electricity, even though the cabins around them had it. I think she liked to visit me just so she could watch television—and because she hoped Sean would be there. She wanted Sean to be her boyfriend. Blech.

As we started down the short, steep bus steps, Sean in front of me, Darcy behind me, someone kicked the bottom of my foot. I slipped on the slick edge of the steps and sat down suddenly just outside the bus. "Hey!" I yelled.

Sean pushed his glasses up and squinted at me like I was some new animal. The bus driver called, "Be careful." Like I fell on purpose. Darcy stifled a laugh. I jumped up, ignoring her outstretched hand, her two colorful friendship bracelets falling onto her palm. Some friend.

"You did that on purpose," I said as the bus groaned away, choking us in diesel fumes.

She ignored me and smiled at Sean. "I'm going to be having a birthday party soon," Darcy said. "You're invited, Sean."

"Oh," he said, still squinting. "Thanks."

I gritted my teeth. "I won't be able to make it," I said. She tossed her head and continued to smile at Sean.

As Sean and I headed up to the park, she called, "I'll send you an invitation, Sean."

"She's a creep," I said. "She invites you in front of me and doesn't invite me."

"So what? You said you couldn't make it anyway," he said.

"You creep," I said and shoved him hard.

But he was laughing. "I don't care about her stupid party."

"She has a crush on you," I said. "She looks at you like Burrito's mother used to look at Mozo.

He grinned. "Well, her ears are kind of long."

We laughed in the wind as it shrieked out of the deeper mountains.

"What if the winds never stop?" I asked Sean.

"Then we'll build kites and fly everywhere," he said.

"That would be fun," I said wistfully as we hiked up the hill.

At the barn, Mama was packing Marigold and Damion outside the barn. When Mama tightened the cinch, Marigold groaned and shifted her weight from one foot to the other and held her breath so Mama couldn't tighten the straps much. That was an old burro trick. You just had to wait until they let out their breath.

"I need you to take these two out to Mr. Bentley," said Mama as she finished lashing down the ropes.

"Aw—why me?" I whined. Actually, taking the burros out to the cabins in the canyon was fun, but I didn't want Mama to know. "It's not my turn."

"You're here, so you'll do it. Don't even *start* arguing, Reba," said Mama. "It won't do you any good."

I sighed noisily.

"I'll go get Burrito," Sean offered.

I took his school books and mine and dumped them on

my bed, then came back outside and helped Mama adjust the cruppers and breastcollars on the two burros. They kept the packs from sliding off a burro's rump or from riding up his neck. Sean returned with Burrito.

"Kane Marshall was here this morning," said Mama.

8

Mr. Bentley's Cabin

My heart nearly stopped beating. "What did he want?" I asked, and didn't dare look at Sean, afraid my gaze would give me away.

Mama gave me a narrow look anyway. "He didn't say at first, but when I told him about the animal in Burrito's stall the other morning, he was very interested."

"You didn't believe me when I told you about it," I said, stubbornly. "You said I was dreaming." How could she act like I was loco, then tell the bounty hunter what I'd said?

Mama didn't respond to that, but said instead, "Kane

Marshall said he was going after an animal that takes large game, like burros, and we should be careful with our stock."

Ice chips ran down my backbone; whether because of the burros' danger or because of the wolverine's danger, I wasn't sure. I thought of the animal book I'd checked out and of the photo of the wolverine, so bold looking, and compared it with real life. My wolverine was bolder than the photo.

My wolverine?

"I want you to be careful," Mama said, and handed me the burros' lead ropes. "Stay on the main trails. The animal Mr. Marshall hunts could have rabies."

"We'll be careful," I said, meekly. It wasn't worth fighting her on this.

Sean took Damion's lead rope. Burrito poked his nose under my arm. I hugged Burrito's shaggy neck as Mama walked into the house, her boot heels clomping on the porch. The screen door banged, and Sean and I set out silently down the dusty road to the trailhead.

How many times had I climbed down this canyon trail? One million? Two million? And somehow the canyon was still new and alien.

"A hummingbird." Sean pointed. A ruby-throated hummingbird hovered over the greasewood, looking more like a mini-flying reptile in its metallic colors. Marigold snatched a mouthful of sage. The hummingbird darted off.

The canyon was cloudy with dust. My eyes filled with it, and I felt half choked. "Mars must be like this," I said and coughed. "Only redder."

"Let's go there," said Sean.

I grinned. "Right now?"

"Maybe we should get our pilot's license first."

"Then Burrito will be the first burro in space," I said.

"He can be uplifted and be the navigator," said Sean. We'd both read these books by David Brin about animals that were uplifted—made smart like people.

Burrito just ambled on beside us, his ears bobbing with each stride. What if he was uplifted, made smarter, more like a human? Would he still be Burrito? Or would he be someone else? I kissed his soft nose and thought I'd rather he stay as he was. Sean said something about mushy girls, but I pretended I didn't hear him.

At the bottom of the canyon we stopped and adjusted Marigold's pack, which was sliding. Mama hadn't tightened it after Marigold had held her breath. Burrito pushed his nose under my arm; *Pay attention to me!* he was saying.

"I love you," I whispered in his long ear and stroked his neck.

"What?" asked Sean from the other side of Marigold.

"Nothing," I said.

Why was it easy to tell Burrito that I loved him, but not Mama, or my brothers (well, I didn't usually love them), or Sean (especially Sean)? I could never tell Sean that I loved him, even though I did. The thought of telling him made my face grow hot.

We walked down to the bottom of the canyon. The river snaked to the east, rocks as big as burros in the water and alongside the stream, as if it had rained boulders.

The trail kept to the west side of the canyon bottom, with the canyon walls rising steeply. Other trails to Devore, West Fork, and even Shortcut (which sounded close but was really far) peeled off at forks. The heat lay heavy in the canyon. *Mars might be like this,* I thought. Hot, reddish, like a monster blowing through his gritted teeth.

We crossed the narrow wooden bridge. Above the bridge was the dam—ugly cement, but necessary when there was much rain. A small amount of water ran under the bridge, light and cheerful. The burros' small hooves rattled over the bridge. When I was younger I had looked for the troll who guarded the bridge. Sometimes, seeing him hiding in a shadow, I'd wave to him.

We passed a cluster of old cabins. Mr. Bentley's was at

the far end. One cabin was surrounded by a high stone wall. The green, peaked roof of the house poked up like an animal's snout and the stone chimney like a cocked ear.

Most of the cabins were summer cabins, already boarded up for the year, because fall was hotter than summer and no one liked the mountains now. You could tell the houses were old because no one built stone houses anymore.

Around a couple of bends—past Bon Accord, the Girl Scout house—the ground was being surveyed. Sean and I had asked the men working and found out that the new vacation homes were actually going to be condos. And they weren't going to be stone, either.

A low wood fence ran around Mr. Bentley's property. Most of his vegetable garden was dead. Lack of water. His garden used to have tomatoes, green peppers, corn, all kinds of stuff. Before the drought, he didn't buy much food; he raised his own and canned it for the winter. He also raised herbs. I liked the anise because it smells like licorice.

Mr. Bentley was sitting on his porch in a straight-back chair with Tristan, his St. Charles spaniel, at his feet.

"Hi, Mr. Bentley," we called. He didn't answer, but we knew he didn't hear very well.

When we reached the gate he just said in his high voice, "Come in and see my house," not even saying hello. Sean and I looked uneasily at each other and the ice chips made my backbone quiver. We tied the adult burros each to a sturdy fencepost.

Marigold held her head up, sniffing suspiciously at the air. Burrito, rolling his eyes, stayed close to the adult burros.

"What's the matter with you?" I asked Burrito, but he didn't follow us. He and Tristan were great friends and would chase each other in the garden.

Sean and I climbed the stairs up the porch. I petted Tristan's soft head. The dignified spaniel leaned against my legs. Mr. Bentley rose. He was thin like an old apple tree and his hand on the top of his cane was shaking.

"What's wrong?" asked Sean.

"Something was here this morning," said Mr. Bentley in his clipped English tones.

My spine grew even colder in the hot canyon.

We crowded behind Mr. Bentley as he threw open the round, Hobbit-like door of his cabin with a bang. Tristan jumped and whined.

"What the heck?" said Sean as we looked inside. The living room was completely trashed.

9

The Mark
of the
Wolverine

What *happened?*" demanded Sean. I said nothing—just gripped the edges of the doorjamb and stared first at the cabin, then back at Mr. Bentley's thin face.

His face was sharp and stern, like the bow of a ship breaking through ocean ice. "Look at my house," he said. "This all happened while Tristan and I took our constitutional." His constitutional was his early morning walk.

A rank scent that I knew all too well drifted out of the door. The wolverine's calling card.

Dirty white stuffing puffed out of ripped couch cushions. All four legs of the two wooden chairs had been bitten off. The starched curtains had been shredded like a giant cat had crawled up them.

Worst of all was his huge bookshelf. It had stretched floor to ceiling, filled with books, tape cassettes, and creeping Charlie plants. Now all of it, along with most of his prized collection of St. Charles spaniel statues of china and glass and pewter, were smashed across the floor. Mixed in with it all was the shattered window glass. The wolverine had simply leaped through the large window in some kind of search-and-destroy mission. Tears burned under my eyelids. Why had he done this?

Could one animal do all this? That horrible smell made it clear that the wolverine had been here. But was there more than one? The book said that they were solitary, except during mating season, which was in the spring.

"This is awful," said Sean. Behind us Tristan whined.

"I'm so sorry, Mr. Bentley," I said. And I did feel sorry, like I was responsible. I had given the wolverine a tortilla, and I hadn't told Kane Marshall what I knew.

Mr. Bentley shot me an odd look. "Not kids. Animal did this," he said. "When I find that beast—" He broke off and shook his fist, his neck stretched like a buzzard's. "I'm setting up traps. I'll catch it. You know what it was after?" He stared first at Sean, then me with narrowed eyes.

We both shrugged, helpless.

"Nothing. Absolutely nothing. It just wanted to tear up my place. I'll get it. I will." Muttering, he went back outside and began to unpack his supplies from the burros.

Sean and I helped carry the food into the kitchen— which, fortunately, was untouched. Only the living room had been ransacked. But that smell filled the whole cabin. The wolverine must have given the living room a good spraying. Sean held his nose. Mr. Bentley saw him and nodded grimly.

After we unpacked Marigold and Damion we started to

help him clean the living room, but he shook his head. "No, you go on. I'll do this. Then I'll set out the traps."

His cold voice made me cringe. Tristan laid his nose on my leg. Maybe he felt guilty that he hadn't been there to protect his master's cabin. But then it was good that he hadn't; a wolverine would surely kill an old spaniel.

We left. I looked back once and Mr. Bentley was holding broken pieces of a china dog. Tears came into my eyes again.

The burros on their way home walked faster, free of their burden. But now I carried a heavy one.

Maybe I really should tell the great white hunter—no, something stopped me. He'd kill the wolverine. Anyway, would the death of the wolverine atone for Mr. Bentley's living room? But nothing would keep the wolverine from striking again, maybe doing something worse.

What if the wolverine really did get Burrito, or one of the other burros? Would I be so protective of him then?

"I—" Sean and I said at the same time.

"You first," he said.

"No, you," I said.

He put his hand on Marigold's withers and brushed off some loose hair. "I think we should tell that hunter guy," said Sean. He didn't quite look me in the eye. "What if the wolverine kills somebody?"

Would he? Of course he could; he was strong and wild enough. But I couldn't believe that the wolverine, free and wild as he was, was all wrong and Kane Marshall, with his rifle and cigarettes and sneer, was right. I shook my head.

"But Mr. Bentley!" Sean was exasperated, his lower teeth showing in a grimace.

"I know," I said, feeling awful. "But I don't think we should tell the hunter."

"Oh, so animals are more important than an old man." Sean glared.

No. Yes. I didn't know. Why was I so reluctant?

Because not telling somehow felt fresh and right, like the clear, clean scent of sage in the morning. I groaned inside. *Get real, Reba, you don't even know why you're protecting it. Sure you love animals, but this one's dangerous. No wonder a bounty hunter is after him.*

Sean and I didn't say anything more. We reached the top of the canyon. The winds had actually stopped. Maybe like the eye of a hurricane. The silence felt odd.

In the barn, Sean helped me groom and put away the two burros. We chased the rest into the barn and fed everybody, still not speaking except to say stuff like, "Get me a halter," or "Marco has a cut, where's the medicine?"

Sean sat a moment on a bale, his hair the same color of the straw. "Are you going to call the hunter then?" he asked abruptly.

I hung up the halters one by one. "No. I can't," I said. And Sean couldn't either, because he didn't have the business card. He had torn his up into the little white pieces that had scattered in the winds.

"You can too," he said and glared.

I shook my head. "No." I just couldn't.

"Then I am."

"But you don't have his business—"

He butted my words aside like an angry burro. "I don't need it. I memorized the number."

I swore at him. If Mama had heard, she'd have grounded me for life.

Sean pinched his mouth, then said, "I'll ask once more. Will you tell him?"

Miserably, I shook my head.

"Just tell me, why not?"

Sean, my friend, don't do this to me.

"Why, Reba?"

I lifted my hands. I didn't know for sure.

"Come on!" he persisted. He almost didn't look like

60

Sean; his eyes angry and hard, someone I didn't know. "Just tell me."

"Because I think that God has a different way." There, I said it. My words hung foolishly like underwear on a clothesline. Intimate, exposed.

"God?" he almost yelled. "Since when do you know—" He broke off and jumped from the bale. He stormed out, running. He ran crunching through leaves outside and was gone.

I stood, wishing stupidly that the winds would blow again, making things more like normal. In their stalls, the burros ate their dinner peacefully. Overhead the sky was streaked copper and gold. Finally I went in the house.

In the kitchen Mama was cooking and Andres sat on the tall stool cutting up hot peppers on the counter.

"Can I help with anything, Mama?" I asked.

"You feed the burros?" she asked. I nodded. "Nothing right now. Thanks, *mi hija*." She stirred a pot of pinto beans on the burner.

Silently I took a tortilla, then had a quick thought and took another. I walked out of the kitchen with Mama's voice calling after me, "Dinner in fifteen minutes."

I hiked up to the stand of knobcone pines where I'd last seen the wolverine. "Why did you do it?" I asked the air.

Nothing.

I asked the question a different way. "God, how do I know what to do? Should I tell the hunter about the wolverine? Or not?"

How do you know if God is talking to you? I'd told Andres that God talked, but now I wasn't so sure. Would he tell me what he wanted?

I had already started down one path—not telling Kane Marshall about the wolverine. "If you really have a different way for me to help the wolverine, please tell me soon, *Señor Dios*." Turn me like a burro feeling the bit pulling on his mouth, telling him to turn the way his rider wants.

Finally I hung both tortillas on the same branch and hiked back along the ridge.

The evening light fell like weighted gold streaks twined with copper and bronze. Mama told me that when I was a baby I would reach for the moon when it was full and tight with silver. Now I held out my hand for a moment, wishing, praying.

Francisco drove up as I stepped onto the porch. The screen creaked as Andres and Miguel bounded outside to see Francisco. They jumped on him, greeting him in loud tones and telling him about school. Like we used to with Papa.

I went into the dark bathroom, shut the door, and sat on the sink. Leaning against the mirror, I closed my eyes and prayed.

10

"Will You Trap Him?"

Tuesday we were on half day at school because of parent-teacher conferences. I thought it was a waste to go at all, and so did most of the kids. On the bus ride home, Sean asked me again, "Are you going to tell him?"

I stubbornly shook my head.

"Reba, why not?" he asked and kicked the seat in front of us. A couple of younger girls squeaked and looked over their shoulders at us. Sean didn't even apologize.

"Because it's not right," I said.

"It's only an animal."

Only an animal. I couldn't believe Sean had said that.

Was Burrito only an animal? If Sean called Kane Marshall, the man would kill the wolverine and not think twice about it.

"Let's compromise," I said. "We can talk to Maury."

Sean rolled his eyes. "Maury is such a weird guy."

I couldn't believe Sean was acting like this.

The bus gave a hard buck over a pothole on the way up the mountain. I clung to the seat edge. "Oh, and the great white hunter isn't weird?" I demanded. "Get serious, Sean. He has a gun, two mean dogs, and he's obviously looking for our wolverine!"

"What are you guys talking about?" asked Darcy. She was just across the aisle from us, next to another girl from our class.

"A video game," I said—just as Sean said, "A movie."

Darcy wrinkled up her freckle-spattered nose. She wasn't a bad kid. I just wasn't thrilled she had such a massive, disgusting crush on somebody who happened to be my best friend.

"So which is it?" she asked, smiling at Sean, who actually smiled back. I could have killed him.

I said, "Actually a movie."

"A video game," said Sean at the same time.

We glared at each other. I *would* kill him.

Darcy laughed. The bus ground to a halt two stops before mine. "Better figure out which it is," she said and got up, lugging a backpack, following her friend. "Bye, Sean." Her voice lingered on his name. I stuck out my tongue at her back.

The bus rolled past her walking home with the other girl; I guess she decided to snitch somebody else's electricity today. She waved up at our window, but Sean was staring at the back of the seat. I saw her, but I didn't wave back. I was curled up inside like a grey pill bug.

Next stop and Sean got up. His stop.

"You aren't going to help me look for the wolverine?" I

asked, a little desperately. I was so sure he'd change his mind.

Sean shouldered his pack. "I'm going to call the hunter, Reba. And tell him what you've seen." His voice was so serious that I wanted to flee like a frightened burro.

But I added, rather nastily, "What you think I saw. You never saw the animal. Not very good evidence."

His back retreated down the aisle. I stuck out my tongue at him, then hunched up in the seat. Outside in the trees, the wind began blowing again—I was glad, for some reason—and dust devils whirled wildly alongside the road. The bus roared up the mountain road.

When I got off at my bus stop, the winds practically pushed me up the hill to the pack station—and I tripped over a rock, not watching where I was walking, because there on the front porch was the great white hunter. He was talking to Mama. I had to blink several times like a traveler in a foreign place to make sense of it.

Mama had on a red-and-brown skirt that rippled around her knees. That meant she'd been down the mountain shopping, or maybe seeing Francisco at one of his restaurants. Usually Mama wore her hair up in a tight braid curled on top of her head, but today it was down, still dark as mine, and it fell to her shoulders in deep waves. Mama had had us young. I think she was just sixteen when Pio was born, and I was struck at how young she truly looked. The great white hunter was looking at her in a way I did not approve.

I marched up to them.

"Here she is," said Mama, putting her hand on my shoulder. I tightened. "Reba, tell Mr. Marshall what you saw the other night."

"But you told him already," I said. Mama's eyes flashed and I knew I was doomed.

"Tell me again," said Mr. Marshall. He towered over us. I had asked God to tug on my reins if he didn't like the way I was going. Was Kane Marshall that tug on the reins? I chilled to that. Would God use this awful man to change my mind? No. I couldn't believe that.

I forced myself to look into his pale blue, humorless eyes and told him, "I'm not sure what I saw that night." And that was true. Mama's hand slid off my shoulder.

"Reba," she warned.

"I didn't see anything for sure," I protested. "I went to the barn because the burros were agitated."

Mr. Marshall shifted his weight. He had one hand in his pants pocket, jingling his coins and keys loudly. "I'm looking for a particularly dangerous animal, Reba" he said, "and I could use your help."

"What kind of animal is it?" I asked.

Mama gave a sigh of exasperation. "Just answer his questions, Reba."

"But I want to know, that's all. Is it a grizzly?" I asked. Mama sputtered.

Mr. Marshall held up his hand. "Kela, it's all right."

Kela. What was this first-name stuff?

Mama smiled at the hunter. I didn't like that smile either. It was bad enough that Francisco got that smile. I frowned at them both.

Mr. Marshall stopped jingling his change. "Kela," he said, "may I speak to Reba alone for a moment?"

Mama shrugged and stalked into the house, the door slamming behind her. I flinched. Mr. Marshall lit a cigarette, but the fire began to build in me.

As the great white hunter smoked, I stared up the hill at the burros. Even in the winds, their manes and tails hardly blew, not like a horse's mane and tail that rippled. The burros were so patient about the heat, the steep hills. A horse would probably colic and have heatstroke at the same time. Burros rarely do. Burros fit in these mountains. Unlike the wolver—

I broke off, hoping he didn't read minds. *Honestly, Reba,* I told myself. *The stupid things you think.*

Mr. Marshall leaned against the porch post, his arms crossed over his chest. He had smooth, defined muscles—too-perfect muscles, like he spent a lot of time working out in a gym. His thinning brown hair flicked in the wind. "Why don't you like me, Reba?" he asked. "I've never done anything to make you not like me, have I?"

My mouth twitched into a frown. "It's not a matter of liking or not liking. You're out to kill that animal and I don't like it."

He laughed low in his throat. "You lay your cards on the table, don't you, girl? You're like your mother in that."

"How do you know what my mother is like?" I almost didn't want the answer.

"Oh, your mom and I go back a ways. We went to high school together. She never would go out with me. Still won't." I was fiercely glad for that. The cigarette smoke danced in the wind.

"We have extreme fire conditions, Mr. Marshall," I said, primly. A tiny slice of my brain was saying, *Don't be stupid, Reba. Go easy. He's dangerous—try to find out more about him.*

He just blew smoke out his nostrils like a fire-breathing dragon. "Tell me what you saw, Reba."

I settled myself like a burro on a tether line. "I didn't see anything clear that night. Something was in the barn. It jumped out the window," I said.

"Your mother told me that your pet had scratches on him." He puffed on his cigarette. His eyes were pale, as if the color had been bleached out.

I shook my head. "My mother thought Burrito got the scratches earlier, when I had him in the mountains."

Mr. Marshall raised an eyebrow. "What do you think?"

"I hadn't noticed scratches earlier."

"And you would immediately notice an injury to your

pet," he said. I nodded reluctantly. But I didn't think the wolverine had scratched Burrito. I figured Burrito had hurt himself on the wooden slats, trying to escape the wolverine.

He added, "And you saw Mr. Bentley's house, didn't you?"

I didn't answer, but the great white hunter smiled when he saw the expression on my face. "See, Reba—that's only a small fraction of what the animal is capable of. You know that. You're a smart girl. You know we're talking about a wolverine, here, don't you?"

Again I nodded, my head not obeying me.

"And you know how clever, how crafty they are, how dangerous they are, don't you?"

I didn't nod that time because I didn't know for sure all that.

"Wolverines don't belong in the San Gabriel Mountains," he said. "They belong farther north. I have no idea how he even got here. They can travel great distances, of course. But how did he even know these mountains were here?"

I asked, knowing he'd deny it, "So you'll trap it and take it somewhere else?"

He dropped his cigarette on the porch and stamped it out with his snakeskin boot. "Wolverines are notoriously difficult to trap," he said calmly. "They sense a trap and even spring them."

His unsaid words hung in the air. I thought of his gun and his dogs and bit my lip. The wind shifted, and one of the burros gave a sobbing bray. I looked up, the wind in my eyes, then into the low chamise, then into an incense cedar tree. Among the olive-green leaves two bright, dark eyes peered out.

11
Setting the Bait

How bold can you get? I asked the wolverine. Wild animals were supposed to be afraid of people. Since I was more afraid of Mr. Marshall than the wolverine appeared to be, I figured I'd better do something.

"Did he escape from a zoo?" I asked the great white hunter in what I hoped were casual tones. I stepped toward the barn, hoping to lure the hunter away. "I need to start cleaning."

He followed me into the low barn, saying, "It's definitely wild."

I began to pitch poop out of the stalls. Mr. Marshall didn't even offer to help. "How do you know?" I asked.

"The L.A. Zoo doesn't report any missing wolverine."

So maybe it came from another zoo—the animal book said that wolverines travel hundreds of miles while they hunt. But it did seem more likely that it was from the Sierras. Maybe even farther. I imagined the wolverine trotting through cities at night, heading south, heading for what? Maybe he had plans to go somewhere specific. Who knew? Maybe they migrated like birds, with maps in their heads.

The great white hunter lit another cigarette.

I couldn't believe this guy. "No smoking from May to December," I said. "National park rules. And no smoking ever in our barn."

"I'm careful," he said, dropping the burnt match to the cement aisle and twisting his shoe on it. What could I do? Fight the cigarette from him? If I was brave I'd hose him down. But even Maury hadn't done that to Mr. Marshall, which told me something.

"Which stall was the burro in who was harassed by the wolverine?" he asked.

"I told you, I don't know for sure what I saw."

"Which stall?"

I thought about lying but he could check easily enough with Mama. Reluctantly I pointed to Burrito's stall.

He went into the stall. I silently set down the pitchfork and left, sliding across the dirt and back into the house, feeling those two eyes burning into me.

At least now I knew what I had to do—entice the wolverine away from Chantry Flat, away from the great white hunter.

"Where's Kane?" asked Mama. She sat on the wooden living-room floor cross-legged, her skirts settled around her, the accounting books before her on our coffee table.

"He's in the barn. I showed him Burrito's stall." I wanted her to think I was cooperating with him. I went into

70

the kitchen and took six tortillas, filled them with cold refried beans and tucked them in baggies. The front door slammed and I jumped nervously.

Out the kitchen window I could see Mama and the great white hunter standing together outside the barn, looking up the hill to the burros. I prayed the wolverine stayed hidden.

Quietly I slipped out the back door and walked around the house. The wolverine was still up in the incense cedar. He peered out from under the flat evergreen needles, swinging his heavy head and staring with his small eyes at us humans. First at Mama and Mr. Marshall, then over at me. Should I try to get him to move, or pray he stayed put?

Sean, on his ten-speed, pedaled through the parking lot toward us. What was this? Him triumphantly telling me he'd called the hunter? No, Mr. Marshall was here—Sean couldn't have talked to him.

But Sean would tell now.

I gripped the tortillas and faded back into the shadows. Now what? Climb the tree after the wolverine? The tortillas in my hands broke in quarters within the baggies.

Sean parked his bike and ran lightly up the porch, the sunlight over his blonde hair like light on seawater. Mama and Mr. Marshall had gone into the barn.

He knocked on the front door.

I took a deep breath and called, "Over here."

He walked over, looking puzzled. "What are you doing?"

To tell or not to tell. I decided in a rush. "The wolverine is here now, and so is Mr. Marshall. But he doesn't know it." Yet.

Sean looked around quickly. "Marshall is going to kill the wolverine," he said.

"I know," I said, puzzled. "That's what I've been telling you."

"But I mean, he doesn't care about anything, except

killing it." Sean didn't quite look me in the eye. "He doesn't want to know why it's here, or anything."

I didn't know why he'd changed, like a burro who suddenly accepts the bit after a long fight. But I was thankful. "There he is," I said softly and pointed to the incense cedar.

He looked, his eyes darkening. "We gotta get it out of here."

"I have an idea," I said, and held up the tortillas. "Can you keep Mama and Marshall in the barn? Maybe show them something?"

"Like what?"

"I don't know. Think of something. I'll try to get this guy to move out of here."

"I'll try," he said. "You be careful of him."

He meant the wolverine. But Marshall was more dangerous.

Sean ran into the barn. His voice piped up. Now it was my turn. I stood under the incense cedar. The wolverine was a good thirty feet up.

"You're crazier than me, you know?" I said softly. "Why are you hanging around here? For kicks?"

He just stared down at me. His fur was like a rich woman's coat. He must be furiously hot.

"Here's something to eat," I said. I climbed a few feet up and laid a tortilla on a lower branch. Then I scrambled down and waited in shadows. The wolverine's nose quivered. He carefully descended, the tree creaking and bits of bark raining down. *Hurry, hurry.* I wanted to jump up and down, but I forced myself to stand very still. Then the wolverine ate the tortilla, one foot on it, neatly tearing up strips.

"And another," I said, draping it on a branch I could reach by standing on my tiptoes.

Hurry, hurry.

The wolverine stretched down and sat on the lower

branch for a long moment, calmly, as if considering what to do next. Sean's voice carried through the open barn window. He sounded concerned. The deeper sound of the great white hunter's voice mixed with Sean's voice. The wolverine snapped up the tortilla. So I put another tortilla at the base of the tree and moved away.

The wolverine stirred, then dropped suddenly off the branch to the ground. I jumped. The wolverine lifted his head to meet my gaze, then took the tortilla in his teeth and ambled away like a dog carrying a newspaper. Something glinted on his throat again. He hopped over a broken stone wall on the other side of our house, his tail flicking in the air and vanished.

I ran after him, jumped on the stone wall, and stood looking. He was gone, completely, like he flew away. I studied the trees around me. Nothing. No leaves stirring, no branches snapping, nothing. Well, that was what I had wanted, wasn't it?

For good measure I set a tortilla down on the far side of the wall. Then I stuffed the rest of the tortilla baggies in my pants pocket and ran back to the barn.

"Here she is," said Sean. He looked so relieved I nearly laughed.

"So you did see this wolverine?" asked Mama. She had her hands on her hips.

"I didn't know what it was," I said. "It ran so fast."

"I was telling them that we looked through animal books to find something that looked familiar," Sean said. "You thought it could have been a wolverine, except they aren't supposed to be around here. So we figured it was an unusual coyote."

The great white hunter held dark fur in his hand; he looked up from it to us, suspiciously. "I'm sure this isn't burro fur," he said. Sean started to argue, but the hunter glared fiercely first at Sean, then at me. "Are you kids playing some kind of game? Because if you are—"

Mama broke in, "Reba, what is going on? Are you not helping Mr. Marshall?"

"We're not playing," I could say that honestly. But I wouldn't help him. I just wouldn't.

Mr. Marshall pocketed the wolverine fur. "Kela, I'll need a pack animal," Mr. Marshall said to Mama. "I'll be hunting for the wolverine and plan to stay out as long as I need to. There've been some sightings by West Fork."

West Fork. That wolverine must bounce around the San Gabriels like a kid in a roller-skating rink.

"When will you need it?" asked Mama. She and Mr. Marshall headed back for the house. Sean and I hastily followed behind them to hear his plans; I prayed the wolverine had stayed out of sight.

"Probably set out on Thursday," he said. "Tomorrow I got some things to do."

Today was Tuesday. Sean mouthed a word at me: Interference.

I found myself saying in my most sensible tone of voice, "Mama, if Mr. Marshall likes I can go along with him." I couldn't bring myself to say *and help*. "School's out after Wednesday because of parent-teacher conference. I know the mountains and I can handle the burro for him."

12
Change of Heart

Mr. Marshall pushed back his hat and looked down at me. I felt like a bug pinned under someone's foot or a trapped animal, except he didn't believe in trapping animals.

"I don't believe I need any help," he said smoothly. I had a shivery feeling that he knew what I'd been thinking. He said to Mama, "Kela, I'll be calling you with the particulars tomorrow."

He turned on his heel and left, boots crunching on dirt.

I sighed. The wolverine was safe—for today at least.

Sean stirred. "I think rain is predicted for later in the week," he said brightly.

Mama looked at him like he'd lost his marbles, which might have been true.

"What's going on here, Reba?" Mama demanded. She'd caught the crosscurrents between me and the hunter, and now she was on a trail of her own.

The trapped feeling vanished and a worse feeling appeared, like being caught in a vise. Mama on the scent was worse than any hunter.

"Reba, I don't want you interfering with Mr. Marshall's work," she said. I started to talk but she interrupted. "I've had enough of your secretive ways. You leave him alone and let him do his job."

I tried to give her a surprised *Who me?* look.

"I know kids like to have secrets and all, but this is nothing to play around with. That wolverine could have rabies."

Rabies. Mama's ultimate disaster. For some parents it was, "Don't you play with that stick, you'll put your eye out." But for Mama it was, "Don't touch that animal. It might have rabies." If even a quarter of the animals Mama warned me about actually had rabies, most of the animal kingdom would be dead now.

"Mrs. Castillo," began Sean.

Mama whirled. "This includes you, too, Sean." Mama turned back to me. "Do you understand me, Reba?"

"*Sí*, Mama." I understood. I'd better not mention the wolverine again, even if he stole all of Mama's underwear.

Sean sat on the stone fence as I went to the country store, slipped under the divider and got sodas out of the refrigerator. Mama didn't mind as long as I kept track. I chalked two hash marks on the tiny message board with my name.

I gave Sean a Dr. Pepper, popped a cream soda open, and sat on the fence next to him. I waited for him to tell me why he had changed his mind. He hummed and the song

76

drifted on the winds. I sipped my soda. "What song is that? It's pretty." I asked.

He gave a sweet smile. "I made it up." He popped open the Dr. Pepper can and drank. He hummed on.

Finally I couldn't stand it anymore and demanded, "So?"

"So, what?"

"Don't make me kill you, Sean. Tell me why you changed your mind."

He pushed up his glasses and stopped humming.

Burrito walked down the hill, swinging his blonde tail, ears up. He liked soda. He pressed his muzzle against the gate.

"I called that Sierra Madre number off the business card." Sean said.

"Yeah?" I would have been scared to call. Sean had guts.

"It was an office. Like real estate," he said.

"Real estate?" Then it clicked. "Mr. Marshall's been hired to clear the way for those new vacation condos," I said, flatly.

Sean gave me a look of respect. "That's it."

Of course. The wolverine would give the condos bad P.R. if he kept up his antics. The builders might have a hard time selling them, or at least getting all the money they wanted.

But why couldn't they just trap him and move him? The animal book had said that wolverines had home ranges. Maybe you couldn't move a wolverine; maybe he'd just go back home like a homing pigeon. Maybe this wolverine had decided Chantry Flat was his home now. Could he have been around longer than I'd realized? Wouldn't I—or someone—have known about him?

He could be shipped to Alaska or Sweden or someplace totally far away, but that would be expensive. Probably something most grown-ups wouldn't want to spend their money on.

"The secretary wouldn't tell me anything at first," said Sean. Burrito rattled the chain-link gate with a small front hoof.

I jumped off the wall and ran to unlatch the gate. Burrito followed me, giving gaspy brays.

"Get ready," I told him. He opened his jaws. I tipped my half-empty can and put it against his lips. He preferred Coke, but he wasn't picky. He gripped the can in his baby teeth and drank, half the soda pouring into his fur, down his chin and throat. "The bees will love you," I told him. He dropped the empty can like a husk and then begged from Sean, flapping his lips.

"No way," Sean told the burro. "I don't want your germs."

Burrito looked at Sean mournfully.

I climbed onto the wall and asked, "So how did you get the secretary to tell you anything?"

"I told her I was friends with Mr. Bentley and about his house being wrecked by an animal," he said. "That loosened her up."

"Smart." I hit my heels against the solid stone.

"I asked what was going to be done for Mr. Bentley and she told me that Mr. Marshall was going to get the animal." He swung his legs like a little kid.

"Why would they care about Mr. Bentley?" I asked.

Sean made a face at me. "Don't you get it? Mr. Bentley is selling some of his property for the new homes."

Oh. I'd seen all the sticks with orange ribbons and lines of string, some near his house, and just hadn't put it together. Or maybe I hadn't wanted to admit that he was selling.

"I asked her if that meant the hunter was going to trap it. I told him that Mr. Bentley had a dog and we didn't want the dog to get trapped."

"Yeah?" I held my breath.

"And she said not to worry. The hunter was going to kill the animal. She never said what kind of animal it was. But I didn't ask either."

"That's what made you change your mind?" I asked.

Sean finally let Burrito have the rest of his Dr. Pepper. Burrito drank it straight down. "Yeah," he said and met my eyes, his gaze direct now. "The wolverine is dangerous. But I think Mr. Marshall should trap it, not kill it. Especially because it's only about money and condos."

I let out my breath. "Now the question is: How can we protect the wolverine?"

We sat and thought. My head was galloping with images: the wolverine in the tree, a gunshot, the wolverine dropping like a fallen kite.

"Not let Mr. Marshall have any burros?" suggested Sean. "No, that's dumb." His blonde hair began to suddenly blow again.

I turned as if to see the person responsible for turning on the wind machine. Behind us Mount Baldy rose clear in the sky, like a blunt rocket. "Mama wouldn't go for that idea," I said. "We have to rent the burros out to pay our bills."

"Maybe we could let the burros out," suggested Sean.

"They don't run away. They just hang around," I told him. "Besides, Mama would figure out it was us who let them go." I didn't tell Sean how badly we needed the money. I'd heard Mama tell Francisco that she was late on her mortgage payment and that the feed bill was overdue, too. I rested my chin on my drawn-up knees.

"Maybe we could lead the great white hunter away somehow," I said. "And somehow keep him from finding the wolverine." Although, the way the wolverine kept hanging around Chantry Flat, Mr. Marshall might not even need a burro to find him.

Sean raised an eyebrow at me. I went on, "Or better—

we can try and lure the wolverine away. Maybe Uncle Hector could help us," I added. Uncle Hector knew a lot. I had just opened my mouth to continue when Burrito suddenly jumped up in the air. I thought maybe a bee had stung him, but just then a clear rifle shot shook the air.

Sean and I bolted for the road.

13
A Shot in the Wind

We ran down the steep dirt hill to the lower parking lot. Off to the left came Maury, running like a scared fox. Mama was at the top of the hill, yelling for me to get over there. But I didn't even slow down.

Sean and I stopped, panting, at the head of the trail, where we had a good view. I felt like a hawk, surveying the land from the top of the canyon. The air smelled only of sage and dryness. I wished I was as sensitive as an animal. Then I could tell who was around by their scent.

Maury pounded up behind us. "Where'd that shot come from?" he asked.

"Maybe it was a truck backfiring," I said, but knew it wasn't. A gunshot and a backfire just don't sound the same.

But at the word "truck," Sean turned and sprinted up the hill.

Maury put his hands on his skinny waist and peered down the curving road. "Don't see nothing," he said. "Maybe a boulder falling? They can crack like a report." He shaded his eyes and studied the mountains.

We were silent, thinking. I was praying, *Please don't let the great white hunter hit the wolverine.*

I already knew what I needed to do, but now I felt it stronger than ever: We *had* to save the wolverine. Somehow. Some way. Mama always taught me: Where there's a will, there's a way.

Sean came flying down the hill on his ten-speed. "Be back in a minute," he hollered.

"I bet he's gonna see if there's anyone down the road with a gun," Maury said. "I'll go check, too." He hurried up to the station for his truck.

We liked Maury a lot. He was only strict on really important things, and he would always explain the rules; he never made us feel like dumb kids. We understood his reasons, so we didn't *want* to disobey. Last year he kept a baby gray squirrel in his office, one that had fallen from its nest. For once Mama didn't say it had rabies. She thought the baby squirrel was cute, too. That little squirrel raced around Maury's office, leaping on and off visitors, making some people yelp with surprise.

Mama came down the hill. She had changed into jeans and braided her hair into respectableness.

She put her arm around me. "You must let Mr. Marshall do his work, *mi hija.*"

She always knew what I was thinking, like my skull was glass and my thoughts shook inside like the colored balls in bingo.

"But Mama," I said, "That means he'll kill the wolverine. He's not even *trying* to trap it."

Mama lifted her face. "This is an odd life, no?" she asked suddenly. "Running a pack station in these desert mountains with one of the biggest cities in the world only a few miles away. I shouldn't be raising a family up here."

"I like it here," I said, stubbornly. Never could I imagine leaving. I didn't mind the trips down to the city—to school, to shop, even to East Los Angeles to visit relatives—because always the mountains were there for us to go home to.

"Caught between two worlds," said Mama. She pushed back her hair. "That's how we are."

"The best of both worlds," I corrected her. She still had a worried look on her face.

"There's other things," she said. "Your papa gone." Her voice caught.

"Oh, Mama." I leaned into her arm and we just stood there. The winds ran through the mountains, lean and swift as hunting cats, springing up the canyon walls, then leaping for the sky.

I moved out from under Mama's arm. "Mama, what if a person feels that she must try to right a wrong?"

Mama gave me a wary look. "What is the wrong?"

"Does it matter?"

"Reba, I don't want you—"

"Mama, please. Mr. Marshall will kill the wolverine. Sean called his office and found out that he is planning on it. We've got to do something." Even talking to Mama, I was shaking.

"What do you care for this animal?" she asked. "This wolverine?"

"I'm not sure," I said, slowly. "Except I do care. A lot. Maybe because it's so clever and crafty, but it still can't defend itself against someone like Mr. Marshall."

Mama made an impatient sound.

"This is important to me, please, Mama," I said. God was tangled up in it, too, but I wasn't sure how to explain that.

Maury's truck rumbled back up the hill. Sean was with him, his bike in the back of the truck.

"I won't have you defying me," she said. "I want you to leave Mr. Marshall alone to do his job."

The winds laughed behind me, tumbling through the canyon. "I can't," I said.

"Reba—"

"I'm serious, Mama. You have to understand."

"I have to, do I?"

I sighed. "But you know what, Mama? I'm not a little kid anymore and I have to do what I think is right."

She started to smile, her eyes exactly like mine, dark and ever so slightly slanted, but changed her mind and frowned. "I know you're not a baby, but you're hardly grown up."

Yet I felt ancient as the mountains.

Mama touched my face. "Reba, I don't want you to get hurt. That is why I worry."

"I know," I said, heavily. I didn't want to get hurt either, but I *was* hurt. I was practically bleeding to death as I stood there. She touched me again, then turned and left me standing at the lip of the canyon.

I stood watching the mountains. I was carved out of stone.

14

The Brown of Drought

I walked back up the hill. Maury had gone inside his office; Sean was perched on the side of the truck bed, waiting for me.

"Did you guys see anything?" I asked.

He jumped from the truck. "Only an empty shell," he said. "Maury has it. It was still warm to the touch."

We hunted around for the wolverine but didn't see him. We didn't see any blood, either. So we headed down the canyon. I hoped the wolverine hadn't returned to Mr. Bentley's cabin.

"I can't lure him away if I can't find him," I muttered,

and sat down on a piece of veined granite. We were off the main hiking trail. We'd doubled back on a deer trail through manzanita, sumac—which we avoided—mountain lilac, and white-thorn scrub bushes. We were below the Chantry Flat trailhead but couldn't see it because of the thick chaparral—prickery shrubs and small trees.

One reason the fire danger was so high is that chaparral, which is practically everywhere in these mountains, is highly flammable. Maury showed me a newspaper article that told how a pound of chaparral has about the same energy as a cup of gasoline. Fire officials had estimated our chaparral at more than 60 tons per acre. "We're talking about the energy of Hiroshima," the fire chief had said. That's why the great white hunter shouldn't smoke in the mountains.

The tortillas and beans squished when I sat down. I'd forgotten they were in my pocket. I pulled them out. The beans had warmed up from my body heat and oozed across the plastic bags.

"Gross," said Sean.

I threw a bag at him.

He dodged, laughing, and the baggie splatted in the dirt behind him. The baggie actually stayed sealed.

I drew lines in the dirt with a stick. "When I was a kid," I said, "I used to think that adults always told the truth and—you know—didn't do bad things. I guess I'm still kind of shocked when they do stuff that's wrong."

The sky transformed into a smoky purple color. The sun had vanished behind the canyon walls.

"I'm going to be late," Sean announced.

We ran, jogged actually since the trail was steep, back up the canyon. At the top, Sean grabbed his ten-speed and swung on.

"Be sure to ask your parents about visiting Uncle Hector," I reminded him. We could look for the wolverine, and maybe we could even spend the night. Last summer we stayed overnight at Uncle Hector's a couple of times.

Sean shot off down the road, his blonde hair the only bright thing in the dusk.

I trudged up the nearly empty parking lot. Because of the relentless heat not many people were hiking. Burrito's thin, piping bray struck the dusk like an organ note, wild and high, vibrating the air. I reached the far end of the barn. The burros were already inside, eating their supper.

The familiar good scent of alfalfa hay wrapped around me. I went in the barn and said hi to Burrito, but he was busy eating and hardly looked my way. So I went back out, and besides the sweetish alfalfa scent there was a strong musky smell.

I sniffed the air like an animal.

Carefully I walked over to the white oak stand, wondering: *Is this an answered prayer?*

The wolverine sat like a dog under the oak trees in the fallen, crunchy leaves. In his mouth was an empty baggie.

I covered my mouth and laughed. "You smart, smart thing," I said. He stared back, like a child gawking. I wondered if he was a young wolverine, even though he looked big to me. Maybe that would explain his destructiveness—he didn't know better. And he also didn't know he should flee from humans.

The front door banged. The wolverine, silent, swift, like evaporating water, shot up an oak—I guess he knew about some humans after all—and vanished in the dark.

The porch boards creaked. "Reba?" Francisco.

I went toward the house. Burrito brayed again, this time not a pure music sound, but harsh and grating. One of the others answered and he was silent. I went into the house.

15

A Bad Game of Checkers

After dinner, as I was playing checkers with Andres, Mama asked us, "Half day tomorrow?"

Andres and I nodded our heads. "Then no school until Monday," I added. Four whole free days. Sheer bliss.

And Mama had said I could go visit Uncle Hector and spend the night. I wished I dared to go look for the wolverine tonight; the moon was just bright enough. But if she discovered I was out prowling around, she'd pitch a fit and might keep me from going to Uncle Hector's. Not worth the gamble.

"Your move," Andres said, twirling one of the checkers.

Francisco sat on the couch with his feet on the coffee table—is there such a thing as a decaffeinated coffee table?—reading the newspaper. Mama was in the kitchen and Miguel was watching an MTV special on AC/DC.

"Don't you have any homework?" Francisco asked Miguel.

I moved my checker. "Gotcha," I said to Andres. "Crown me." He made a horrible face.

"I did my homework already," said Miguel. He turned the volume higher with the remote.

"Let's see it," said Francisco.

Miguel sighed. "It's in my locker at school. I did it during last period."

Francisco put down the newspaper. "I find that hard to believe."

Miguel gave him a furious look, but said, "Why?"

"I'm just surprised you don't have more work in high school, that's all," said Francisco.

"Well, I don't," said Miguel.

Andres shuffled his feet and moved his checker. He made a bad move again. "Are you sure you want to do that?" I asked. Andres frowned and put his fingers back on the checker. Illegal, but I kept my mouth shut.

"Miguel gets good grades," said Andres, suddenly, to Francisco.

"Does he?" asked Francisco. He didn't sound the least bit convinced. Miguel carefully set down the remote and stalked out of the room.

Andres moved his checker. Not a good move; I was able to crown another of my checkers.

"Dang it," said Andres. He started to move one of his checkers when Francisco leaned over.

"Think, Andres," said Francisco. "Is that a good move?"

Andres took his hand off the checker and chewed his lip. I wished Francisco would go back to his newspaper and leave us alone. Andres slid the checker back and forth over the squares. If he wasn't careful, I'd be able to crown another checker. But I knew better than to say anything helpful to him. He was getting that murderous look in his eye.

Andres slid the checker to a square. Francisco boomed with laughter. Andres looked up at me with hurt eyes. I nodded a tiny nod—bad move. Andres sprang up, knocking all the checkers to the floor, and ran off.

Two down, three to go. Francisco looked after Andres, puzzled, as if he really didn't know why he'd exploded. I began to pick up checkers.

Dishes clattered in the kitchen. I wanted Mama to come and tell Francisco to stop, but I knew she'd side with Francisco.

I folded the checkerboard and put the checkers in a baggie. I turned down the volume of the TV.

Then I looked at Francisco. He tried a small smile. I knew, deep down, that he didn't mean to be insensitive, but I couldn't stop myself from saying, "So what are you going to say to make *me* run out of here?"

Francisco rubbed his chin. "Reba," he began, but I stood up. Part of me felt just a twinge sorry for him, but the other part of me—no way. He had to figure it out himself.

Mama came out of the kitchen, wiping her hands on a dish towel. "Where are the boys?" She looked at me. "Reba?"

"Ask him," I said and walked out, the checkerboard under my arm. I went into my room and shut the door. One of the few advantages to being the only girl: I got my own room. I shoved the window frame up and leaned on the sill.

The winds trickled inside, blowing papers on my desk. Overhead the moon, lopsided like a drunk old man, gleamed orange in the dusty night sky.

91

Guilt pricked at me like cactus quills. I'd been deliberately cruel to Francisco.

Okay, but he'd been mean to us, on purpose!

But I knew I wasn't seeing the truth of it.

Besides, a little cactus voice pricked me and said, *Are you in charge of dispensing justice?*

Sure, why not?

Then right your own wrongs!

My muscles twitched and I couldn't take my eyes off the moon.

16

Confetti and Sparkle Day

The next morning, Wednesday, I rushed around getting ready for school. The teachers would no doubt load us with homework to make up for missing two whole days.

I burst into the bathroom. Pio, my oldest brother, was examining his face in the mirror. I lined my toothbrush with paste, the kind with blue sparkles.

"Reba," Pio said. "What's with you and Francisco? Mama told me that you were causing trouble last night."

I deliberately shoved the toothbrush into my mouth so I couldn't answer. I was causing trouble? Not exactly.

Pio smeared shaving cream on his jaw, glancing at me every few seconds. With careful strokes he began to shave.

When I'd brushed each tooth about fifty million times, I said through the foam, "Francisco was being cruel to Andres. Making fun of him playing checkers badly. And he was picking on Miguel. I was gonna be next."

Pio shrugged. "Francisco is an okay guy. He was just trying to help."

I flared. "He wasn't helping. Andres was ready to cry."

"Andres is too sensitive," said Pio. "He should tough up."

"Francisco wasn't toughing him up. He was making fun of Andres." Though as I said it, I knew that Francisco wasn't trying to be cruel; he was just awkward with feelings, like a burro being packed for the first time. He wobbles and bumps into everything.

"Well, I like Francisco. He's good for Mama." Pio ran hot water on his razor.

I put my toothbrush in the holder and started out of the bathroom, wondering if I was awful to wish Pio would cut his throat with that razor.

"Now there's you," Pio called as I went into the hallway. The overhead light bulb was dim with cobwebs. "We're all worried about you. You're acting so weird."

I paused, amazed. I was acting weird?

Pio reached out and grabbed my arm. He hauled me back into the bathroom and shut the door. I struggled, but he didn't let go.

"Look, Reba. Mama deserves some slack. She's finally found someone who likes her and she likes him. Quit making it hard on her."

I jerked my arm free. "What about Papa?"

"Oh, please," said Pio. He stuck his shaving stuff in the drawer.

I rubbed my arm where he'd gripped it. "He might come back," I said.

Pio opened the bathroom door and stomped out. "Grow up, Reba. For goodness sake, grow up."

School was wilder than usual, kids acting goofy up and down the halls. I lost myself in the madness and forgot home for a while.

Our teacher did assign us a ton of homework, but she also let us make *cascarones*, eggshells with confetti inside, instead of having English.

To make *cascarones*, you poke two holes in the shell and blow out the insides. Then you poke one of the holes bigger and fill it with tiny colored confetti and silver and gold sparkles. Then with glue and white tissue paper you reseal the hole. Everyone made several eggs. Then with felt-tip pens we decorated the shells.

Then just before school let out, we cracked the eggs over the heads of our favorite people. Kids ran up and down the aisle. Even our teacher laughed and ran a little bit, like a kid.

Of course, Darcy cracked both her eggs on Sean's head. She was so disgusting. I cracked one of my eggs on his head and the other eggs on girlfriends. I cracked the *cascarone* with the wolverine drawing on Sean's head. I showed it to him first, and he yelled, "We'll save him yet!"

Then the last bell rang and we all ran for the bus, trailing bits of sparkle and rainbow colors.

"When can you go see Uncle Hector?" I asked Sean, as we settled on the bus seat.

"Just tonight through Thursday." I was disappointed. I'd hoped we could stay until Friday. Mama didn't need me until the weekend to help with the country store and the burros.

Sean lowered his gaze. "My parents say I spend too much time with you."

I sighed impatiently. Just as Mama thought most wild

animals had rabies, so Mr. and Mrs. Evans thought too much of me was bad for Sean. That stung.

"I'm bad for you?" I asked.

"No," he said and lifted his head, looking into my face. His eyes were the color of the pool at the bottom of Sturtevant Falls, grey-blue.

"Why do they say that then?"

He sighed. "When I'm rude at the table or something, sometimes Mom says I get the rudeness from you." I started to blurt an angry response, but he interrupted. "I think for all her psychology stuff, she doesn't want to admit I'm just rude because I *am*—no thanks to anybody."

We laughed together, even though his words still stung.

"But I got the real reason out of them last night," said Sean, and he paused.

"What?" I asked, my brown fingers curling around the edge of the hard plastic seat.

"I don't believe this way at all, but my parents do."

"What?" I asked again, but a sick feeling in my stomach told me I knew what he was going to say.

"It's because you're Mexican and I'm white."

I leaned back in the seat, deflated as a broken *cascarone*. The blue, yellow, green, red, and purple colors and the silver and gold sparkles had fallen to the ground.

"But we aren't different, are we?" I asked, and looked at his hands, light tan. My uncle had married a white woman and I had stopped seeing her color long ago.

"You're my friend forever," he said earnestly. I thought he was going to touch my arm, my hair, my face, but instead he sat back with a sigh.

His words did make some of the sting go away.

"Well," I said, trying to be cheerful, trying to forget about his mother, "we'll have today and tomorrow at Uncle Hector's and maybe we'll figure out a way to lure the wolverine away."

He nodded his bright blonde head. "I'll see you in about an hour. My mom said she'd drive me up."

He hopped off at his stop and walked into the wind.

At home only Mama was there. Pio and Miguel were still at school. Andres had gone to play at a friend's down the hill in Arcadia.

Uncle Hector had no phone, but he always seemed to know when someone was coming to visit, so I didn't feel bad dropping in. He always welcomed Sean and me.

"Take this to Uncle Hector," said Mama. She was letting us use Serrano, a bright chestnut with flaxen mane and tail. Mama handed me a sack of canned vegetables and fruit, pinto beans, and a bag of flour to pack on Serrano for Uncle Hector.

Uncle Hector wasn't really my uncle—just an old man who lived out in the mountains, farther than most people. He raised some cattle, some chickens, had an occasional llama or two, and knew a lot about the Gabrielino Indians. He told everyone he was part Gabrielino, too, though Pio's college anthropology professor said that there are no more Gabrielino Indians, that they died out a hundred years ago like an endangered animal species or something.

"Reba," said Mama as we tightened the straps on Serrano's harness. "Remember what I said about staying out of Mr. Marshall's way."

"I know," I said, heavily.

"Reba—he's being paid to do this, you know that? It's not just for fun. It's his job."

Don't tell me he doesn't enjoy it, I thought.

"And the longer it takes him, the more the people who hired him will have to pay. And they won't be happy about that. They don't care about the wolverine one way or the other. They just want it gone. And I can't say I blame them. Remember when the bears came down to Sierra Madre a few years ago? They had to kill one of them."

But bears roaming the city streets was different than a

wolverine in our canyon, wasn't it? Killing him just didn't seem fair. Okay, he did cause Mr. Bentley plenty of grief, but was that reason to kill him?

Oh, why did you do that? I asked. But no answer came.

"Go see Uncle Hector," Mama said kindly. "He's a good man."

Sean's mom drove up in her seal brown Jaguar and Mama went to talk to her. Sean climbed out with his daypack. We didn't need much to go to Uncle Hector's—just a change of clothes. For a moment I watched Sean's mom and Mama talk, both smiling. Sean's mother had short blonde hair and wore lots of makeup. I wondered what Sean's mom thought of Mama.

"Ready?" asked Sean.

"Almost," I said to Sean. "First I gotta write a letter."

17
Wolverine Perfume

What letter?" Sean asked.

"I'll show you." We sprinted for the house, Serrano peering after us.

"Take the phone book," I said, tossing it to him. I sat at my desk in my bedroom; Sean sat on my bed.

I pulled out notebook paper. *"The Pasadena Star News,"* I said. "I'm going to tell them about the wolverine and us and Mr. Marshall."

"For insurance?" said Sean.

"Exactly." I wrote fast.

Dear *Pasadena Star News* Editor:

There is a wild wolverine living in the San Gabriel Mountains.

A man named Kane Marshall is going to kill it because certain people are afraid the wolverine will bring down the price of the new cabins. We are trying save the wolverine.

Sincerely,

Reba Castillo, 12
Sean Evans, 12

"There!" I read it out loud. We signed our names. I asked, "What's Mr. Marshall's phone number?" Sean, with his perfect memory, told me, and I wrote it down so the newspaper could check our story. *If* the office would tell the truth.

"You should add that the best thing to do for the wolverine is to trap it. Something Mr. Marshall isn't willing to do," said Sean.

I added the P.S. and searched for an envelope and stamp. We ran over to Maury's office because he goes to Arcadia to do his shopping. He promised to mail our letter. He looked like he was going to ask what it was, but decided to wait until we wanted to tell him. Maury was nice like that.

"We're going to Uncle Hector's," I told him on the way out the door.

"Wish I could go," said Maury with a sad smile. "I love his hot tub."

For all Uncle Hector's old Indian ways, he'd built himself a hot tub, heated by solar energy. He said it was like the Indians' sweat huts.

We trotted back toward the barn. Serrano pawed with his front hoof, his ears straight up, his nostrils flaring. "You old goat," I told him. Suddenly Burrito minced out of the barn, his little hooves clattering on the cement.

"How did you get out?" I turned to Sean. "Did you let him out?"

Sean was looking past my head. "Not me," he said. "Looks like they're all out."

I whirled around. All the burros were spilling across the park, meandering among the picnic tables.

"Mama!" I bawled.

She ran out of the house. The three of us ran up the hill where the burro gate was sprung.

"Who did this?" said Mama crossly.

Our eleven burros didn't go far. Most of them fell hungrily on the patches of grass between picnic benches. We grabbed sticks and chased them back into the pasture. A few mothers and their kids were in the park. They stood on the tables, laughing and pointing at the burros.

"Reba, did you leave the gate—" Mama began.

"No!" I'd been careful, as always.

Mama frowned. "Then how—" She broke off as the wolverine trotted across the park, bold as the dark, leisurely as an old man out for a walk. He vanished in a dense thicket of manzanita on the ridge.

"A doggie! A doggie!" shrieked one of the kids.

One of the mothers walked over to us, a baby on her hip, a little kid at her side. "Was that a bear cub?" she asked.

Mama shook her head. "Wolverine," she said grimly.

"It stinks," said one of the kids.

"It's wolverine perfume," I told him as the winds came through and stirred the smell all over the park.

"Smells bad," said the kid firmly. I had to agree with him about that. But then I think some expensive perfume smells bad, too.

After we chased all the burros back, they milled around agitatedly in their pasture. Most of the other times the wolverine had been around, he'd been downwind from them.

Sean walked back down the hill. "The wolverine's gone," he shouted.

Mama was frowning as she examined the gate latch. A latch of metal with a bolt stuck through a ring to hold the latch in place. The bolt was on the ground. I picked it up and handed it silently to her. She locked the latch. No way could the wolverine have let the burros out, could he?

Sean was on his knees in the dirt, examining the chain-link fence next to the gate. "Fur," he said. "Doesn't look like burro fur, either."

We crouched down. Sure enough, black fur clung to the rough edges of the chain link. Fur that was thick and silky.

"The wolverine let them out," I said. Mama and Sean stared at me. The burros could have pulled the bolt; they were smart enough. But the gate was built so that from the inside they couldn't reach the bolt. Someone outside had to do it. Or some animal.

Mama went off into a Spanish lament. She came back into English and said, "I'll get a lock. Surely that animal can't do a combination lock." She gave me a look that said she didn't believe the wolverine had released the burros, but she wasn't quite sure either. But in my mind I could see the wolverine unlatching the gate.

Sean, Mama, and I went back to Serrano and Burrito, who stood under the arch of Serrano's neck, protected.

We finished packing Serrano with our gear. His load was light compared to what he often had to pack. I kept looking around but didn't see the wolverine. Mama came back out with more canned food for Uncle Hector and packed it.

"By the way, where are all my tortillas?" she asked.

"They are so good, Mama," I said. The wolverine thought so too.

"Are you going to tell Mr. Marshall about the wolverine and the burros?" asked Sean, seriously.

"What is there to tell?" she asked lightly. "One of us

didn't latch the gate properly this morning. We saw the wolverine again, yes, but he disappeared so quickly."

Mama was on our side! Or, at least, she wasn't willing to be against us.

"Thanks, Mama," I said gratefully.

"For what?" she snapped. "Now go to Uncle Hector's. And be careful."

We circled the park once more before we left, but the wolverine had vanished, like he'd dropped into a black hole.

Uncle Hector lived way out by West Fork. It wasn't a difficult hike—first along the Gabrielino Trail, then onto the Silver Moccasin Trail. As we went down the canyon from Chantry Flat, I dropped pieces of tortilla with beans along the way.

"Like Hansel and Gretel," said Sean.

"If only the birds don't eat all the pieces," I said. "I don't think the wolverine would care to follow little white stones."

"Do you suppose the wolverine can't find his way home?" asked Sean.

"Maybe," I said. "We have to help him to a safe place." That's what everyone wanted, wasn't it? A safe place. Did Mama need a safe place, too? Was that what Francisco was?

Burrito started to lip up the tortilla, so I whacked him on ahead of me.

The wolverine didn't show up. But we did see little sparrows flock down and snatch the tortilla pieces.

18

The Pawprint of God

Uncle Hector's place was about ten miles over twisting trails.

"But we're tough," I said as we panted up a hill. The sun flooded the mountains with hot gold.

"Well, tough most of the time," said Sean, and he wiped the sweat off his forehead.

"Look at the bushes," said Sean. On the north side of the ridge along the narrow trail grew clumps of sugar bushes, Spanish bayonets, mountain lilacs, and the everpresent manzanita. "They look white," he said. "How weird."

We peered at the odd-looking, pale bushes. Serrano

chomped some of the least weird-looking ones, and the scent of sage from the crushed and chewed leaves washed around us. Burrito nuzzled my arm and I petted him.

"It's blighted," I said. "Maury said this fungus is killing a lot of the chaparral because the drought has weakened the plants."

"How awful," said Sean. "I wish the rain would come."

"I know."

We walked on. The blighted plants were especially bad up here. The burros curled their nostrils at the greyish-white fungus and didn't steal bites.

"It's like, 'Come on, God—do something,'" I said.

"Why should God?" asked Sean.

I looked at him in surprise. "Because he's God. God is supposed to help."

"So he's responsible for this?"

"Well, no, but he can make it better," I said.

"He hasn't yet. So, maybe there isn't even a God," said Sean.

I had wondered, too—especially when Papa left. "No," I said, slowly. "There is."

"But how do you know?" he said. We crossed a thin trickle of the stream. The burros drank deeply, standing fetlock deep in the lukewarm water. Sean and I sat on big stones in the stream to rest.

"I just know," I said. "It's like imprinted inside me or something."

Sean asked, "So who's *causing* the drought? God?"

I wondered about that, too. Did God make stuff happen to punish us? Was he punishing me by having Papa leave?

"No," I said again, not quite sure. "I don't think he's punishing us. I think it's more like we're doing it to ourselves. Like the ozone layer is messed up because people used the wrong chemicals. Maybe the drought is like that, too."

106

"But *I* didn't do that," said Sean. "And the animals didn't either. Why are they suffering? Why should the sage bushes suffer for something they didn't do?"

"I don't know," I said. Sean was right; it wasn't fair. Mama always told me that life isn't fair. But shouldn't God *make* life fair? I stroked Burrito's narrow face. "I think God wants to help us, he just can't come in and change everything."

"Why not? He should," said Sean. He had that look he got sometimes, like he was going to bust out crying—except he hardly ever did. He just got that look.

I put my hand in the water and stirred. Dirt and gold flecks stormed in the ripples. "Because if God just came in and fixed everything, we'd be like spoiled brats, always wanting our own way and never learning anything. Just like if your parents never let you get in trouble for any stupid things you did."

Burrito splashed over and peered up into our faces, as if trying to figure out what we were quarreling over. He looked around as if to say, *No food to fight about here. Can't be that.* He gave a questioning half bray. We both patted him to reassure him, but he continued to watch us uneasily.

"Better go on," I said. Sean got up and held out his hand. I let him pull me to my feet. Not because I needed him to, but to accept his apology. Not that he even had to do that. I couldn't blame him for wondering if there was a God. I knew there was, but I couldn't even explain how I knew. Maybe it was just that, if there was no God, nothing made sense.

And I hoped that Sean would see that some day. Probably, deep in Sean's heart, there was a little print, like an animal track, that showed that God had been there—and would return if Sean wanted him to.

19

The Medicine Hat Horse

We climbed a small rise where the winds snapped fiercely, then on down through a cluster of scrub oaks that held back the winds, which impatiently rattled the leaves and gusted in our faces. We stopped again to rest and to drink the last of our water from the canteens that Serrano carried. A dry riverbed ran to the east of our path. Big granite boulders rested between trees, sparkling black and white in the sunlight.

We hiked for a long time, careful to take the path that nearly doubled back on itself, rather than the trail to Mount Wilson. When we saw DeVore Campground—picnic tables,

109

outlined areas to camp in—we turned north for Uncle Hector's. My legs were aching.

Dusk was settling in with orange and red stripes. The air had turned cooler. We had climbed over a thousand feet.

Suddenly, a large yellow dog with blue eyes loped up to us from out of a bunch of sage.

"Rufus!" I shouted, and flung myself at the dog. Burrito rushed over, eager. Rufus licked my ear and Burrito's face, and then swiped at Sean's hand and sniffed Serrano cautiously. With dignity, the old burro raised his head, and the two animals acknowledged one another as equals. Then Rufus turned and ran back the way he came.

"To tell Uncle Hector," said Sean, and he laughed.

"I can hardly wait to get into the hot tub," I said. "My legs are so tired."

"Mine too. We should let Burrito in," said Sean. "I bet he's tired."

The pale burro baby wasn't moving with his usual sparkle. But then none of us were.

As the sky purpled, Uncle Hector's cabin appeared over a rise. A modest adobe cabin. Uncle Hector had built it himself. We ran the last few yards in. Even Serrano trotted, his packs bouncing madly. Uncle Hector stood in the open doorway, smiling, hands on the doorjamb.

"Hi, Uncle Hector! Hi, Uncle Hector!" Sean and I shouted happily.

He held out his arms. We ran to him and he embraced us both. He smelled like sage and heat, like the mountains themselves.

"I knew it was someone I liked very much," he said. "Rufus came back yipping and smiling." He pulled at our arms. "Come in, come in."

"Can we put the burros in the barn?" I asked.

"In the pasture," he said. "The small pasture. I'll show you the barn in a moment."

That had a funny ring to it. "What's wrong?" I asked.

"I'll show you in a minute," he said, but wouldn't explain.

The sunlight was finally gone, and the mountains were dark as a well. Stars shone out like the inquisitive eyes of wild animals. Yet Uncle Hector walked without a flashlight, the land familiar under his feet. Sean and I clung to Serrano. Burros have good night vision.

"Here's a small spring where they can drink," said Uncle Hector. "I don't even have enough water in the well for them. All the wild animals come here to drink," he said. "Deer, bear, coyote, raccoon, I see them all. It's the only water around for miles."

The spring was in his small back pasture against a low hill. The water seeped out into a pool the size of a kids' plastic wading pool. Stars quivered on the water. Burrito and Serrano drank, making sucking noises. I put my hand lightly under Burrito's throat, feeling the gulps of water go down.

Overhead, bats—whose usual sonar sounds are much too high for us to hear—cried in high voices. Maybe they were telling us to stay out of their way. The darkness was their friend. But I was still a little afraid of the dark. I pressed against Burrito, who nuzzled me wetly. Then we led the burros back to the light of Uncle Hector's windows and unpacked Serrano.

"Lovely, lovely," murmured Uncle Hector, examining the canned goods Mama had packed. "Your mother is an angel."

"Sometimes," I admitted.

He laughed. "Anyone is an angel from a distance, no? It's up close they become devils."

We took the burros back to the pasture near the cabin and turned them out with his medicine hat horse. Burrito gave a halfhearted buck in the light from the cabin, then he and Serrano began grazing the meager grass, ignoring the horse, who stared widely at them. The medicine hat horse was mostly white with red flecks and a red mark between his

111

ears. Indians believed that a horse marked that way was sacred, that neither bullet nor arrow could harm the horse or its rider.

We walked back to the cabin. "Uncle Hector," I said. "Where are your other animals?"

He took a battery lantern from the kitchen table and we walked out toward the barn, with Sean and me on either side of him. "I had to sell all my cattle," he said quietly.

"Oh, no," Sean and I said together.

Uncle Hector raised the prettiest purebred Angus cattle. Solid black, with curly fur on their foreheads. He sold the calves to kids for 4-H projects.

"Not enough water," he said. "I sold my llamas too."

"And the medicine hat horse?" I asked. "Are you going to keep him?"

"He's my transportation."

I was glad for that. The medicine hat horse seemed like part of the family. But then so did the cattle and the llamas. I wanted to cry for the sadness of it.

"If the rains don't come soon," said Uncle Hector, "I fear that when I buy back my llamas, they won't know who I am."

"Should we be here?" I asked suddenly. "I don't want us to drink all your water."

"No," he said and hugged me. "You're all right. I need visitors. But no hot tub."

We groaned.

"I'll give you both rubdowns instead," he said.

When Uncle Hector worked as a Thoroughbred horse trainer, he used to rub down his horses' legs. He did a good job on people, too.

"Now my barn. I want to show you something," he said. The lantern light flooded the outside of the low barn built from adobe bricks that Uncle Hector had made himself. Once when I was up on my Sunday hill I had read in the Bible about when the Hebrews were in Egypt; the Pharaoh

112

had them make mud and straw bricks. Just like Uncle Hector.

He opened the barn door. "See?"

An all-too-familiar scent swarmed out.

"Oh, no," Sean and I said together. Uncle Hector gave us a long look.

"The wolverine," I explained with my eyes watering. Bales of hay were shredded and kicked around the barn. There were bite marks in the stall dividers. Some of the leather bridles and halters had been chewed, leaving pieces of leather looped over the floor like entrails.

"He perfumed my barn, mostly," said Uncle Hector. "What do you know of this *comadreja*, this weasel?"

Again I wondered if I was doing the right thing, trying to protect this animal who was causing so much trouble.

The night winds howled behind us and Sean touched my hand. There was something big astir in the mountains. I think we all could feel it.

20
The Hidden Spring

We went back to his cabin where he gave us cups of precious water to drink. I sprawled in front of the empty fireplace on a rug dyed fiery red and jewel blue, woven from llama wool. Sean lay on his back on my right side and Rufus snored on the left.

"So what do you know of this wolverine?" asked Uncle Hector. He sat in his handmade wooden rocking chair with a cup of spearmint tea, from past herb gardens, and rocked back and forth on the packed dirt floor.

"That's why we're here," I said. Uncle Hector raised his eyebrows. We took turns telling him about the wolverine

115

and the great white hunter and why the wolverine was wanted dead.

"Building more houses, huh?" he said. "Progress is important, but it must be done in a proper manner." He went quiet with thought and rocked slowly back and forth in his straight chair. I fell asleep on the llama rug and dreamt of an uplifted wolverine and me piloting a spaceship. But no matter how hard we looked, we couldn't seem to find outer space.

Thursday morning I woke to the sound of a gunshot.

I sat bolt right up. I was alone on the llama rug. I called but no one was in the cabin, so I ran outside and Burrito cried out to me and rushed up to the fence. Uncle Hector and Sean were at his well, pumping water.

"Was that a gunshot?" I asked, my heart pounding harder than it should.

Uncle Hector gave me an inscrutable look and said, "I believe so."

"We couldn't tell exactly where it came from. The winds are blowing the sound around," said Sean.

I stood nervously. Uncle Hector gave Sean the bucket of water, then he took my arm and led me into the burro's pasture and up to the spring we'd visited last night.

"Examine these prints," he said. "For you will track them today."

I dropped to my knees and stared at the damp soil that seethed with the mountain water.

"See the wolverine's print? How large it is? And see his five toes?" said Uncle Hector. "But sometimes his small toe does not show. Perhaps he's been injured."

"He drinks here?" I asked, astounded that the wolverine traveled so fast and so far. It was almost like magic.

"It's the only water around," said Uncle Hector.

"Have you seen him?" I asked.

"From a distance." Uncle Hector pointed out the wolverine's tracks. "He's trotting here." Two paw prints almost next to each other, then a leap of space, then two more.

One track led up the hill and around behind the spring. "He was searching and checking. Curious animal," said Uncle Hector. He also pointed out other animals' tracks, many I knew already, who came for the water: the mule deer with their two curved prints, like half moons; the raccoon with his long, monkey-like toes; the coyote with his four toes and large back pad.

"I used to see an occasional wolf," he said.

"What happened to them?" I asked.

He shrugged. "They don't like people. They left years ago."

Animals were smart. They knew to leave when it was time. I twisted some of my hair, thinking. Did Papa know he had to leave? Was he like the wolf, having to move on?

Then Uncle Hector described the mountain lion's track. "Big, three, sometimes four inches long. Sometimes I hear the lions scream at night," said Uncle Hector. "They come all the way down here from the Sierra Nevadas when hunting is poor. As the wolverine has done, I think."

"If I can find him, and track him, what should I do next?" I asked.

Uncle Hector smiled. "That part is up to you."

Except that I didn't know what to do.

Back at the cabin, we washed with the water Sean brought in from the well and ate a breakfast of eggs, courtesy of Uncle Hector's chickens. No milk—the pretty Jersey he'd used for butter and milk was gone, too. Uncle Hector spread out a map on the rough wood table and we studied it.

"We should take the wolverine here," said Sean, pointing to the big, open San Gabriel Wilderness Area. "He won't bother people there." No one lived in the wilderness area, of course—it was a protected area. No vehicles allowed.

"Is there water there?" I asked Uncle Hector.

"I imagine some," he said. "It's higher up and catches what little rain climbs over the peaks."

So. Track the wolverine, find him, take him to the wilderness area.

But even if I found him, how would I get him to follow?

My thoughts ran back to Noah and the ark. How the heck did Noah get all those animals in the ark? If he could do that, then couldn't I move one wolverine?

We filled our water bottles with well water and I stuffed tortillas and dried prickly pear fruit, presents from Uncle Hector, in my pockets.

"Be careful," said Uncle Hector. "If you're not back here tonight, I'll go out after you."

"Why not come with us now?" I asked impulsively.

Uncle Hector's dark, creased face smiled. "I'd love to, *mi hija*, but I think this is your quest."

So Sean and I walked across the pasture to the spring to pick up the tracks. The early morning light shone over the mountains like thin, fine gold. Burrito cruised behind us.

When we jumped the stone fence, Burrito called his longing to us. "We'll be back," I told the little burro. He bobbed his long ears and brayed his anguish at being left behind.

The wolverine prints wound around the spring, then headed west, the opposite direction from the wilderness area. Beyond the spring, the tracks were hard to follow because the ground was baked hard. In places of deep dust, a print or two would show up.

"Is that one?" I'd asked.

"I think it's a deer track," Sean would say.

"Deer don't have toes!"

So we argued our way along what we hoped was the wolverine's path. The truth was, I felt discouraged. How much would I be able to do in one day? Sean would have to go home or face the wrath of his parents. But I could keep looking. We had enough food and water in our daypacks for a couple of days—Uncle Hector had made sure of that.

The sun was muted overhead, veiled behind high clouds. The winds muttered over the mountains in a furious undertone.

About noon, we sat down to rest and to think. The tracks vanished between two large boulders of granite. We sat in the shade of one of the boulders.

"This is stupid, isn't it?" I said.

Sean shrugged. "We have to try."

I leaned against the rock. "Even if we find the wolverine, how are we going get him to do anything?"

"I don't know." Sweat had darkened Sean's green tee-shirt.

Maybe we should just go back to Uncle Hector. No, I couldn't. Not yet.

The winds slowed, and a faint gurgling sound trickled out from between the rocks. I got up. "Is that water?"

We squeezed between the boulders. Down the hill was a merry stream running quietly through a dense forest of pines and oaks. A pool of water was hidden from the thin trail by the rocks and trees. If I hadn't heard the soft sound of water, I would never have known it was there.

Birds trilled and sang. Some jays squawked around. The animals must love this place. We took off our shoes and soaked our feet in the cold water.

The pool wasn't much bigger than Uncle Hector's hot tub, but it was deep and icy cold.

"I wonder if Uncle Hector knows about this," I said.

"He must not, or he could have brought his cattle up here," said Sean.

"We'll have to tell him," I said. "Then he can buy back his animals."

We stood quietly, knee-deep, enjoying the wetness, when suddenly the birds fell silent. Even the wind seemed quieter. I stared at Sean, suddenly afraid even though the jays hadn't screamed an alarm. Sean jerked his chin, motioning behind me. Slowly I turned in the water.

The wolverine was sitting on the bank, watching us. The pale brown stripes on his sides were the color of Burrito. His tail lay behind him, as forgotten as a backpack.

I jumped as a loud crashing came from the northwest, startling me.

The wolverine calmly waded into the water, his dense fur floating on the water's surface.

Wolverine Trio

The wolverine swam toward us like an otter, his small round ears cupped forward.

More crashing came from behind the trees. I gripped Sean's arm. No animal, not even a bear, made that much noise. "The great white hunter is coming," I whispered. "We've got to hide." We pulled our packs off and hid them in bushes.

Then I held my breath and ducked under the water. The cold shot through me and I wanted to scream, but I chased the sound back inside. Sean plunged under and together we swam underwater toward a shadowed area.

Gold and green slants of light penetrated the pool. Little grey fish shot by in small schools, moving together like dancers. I kicked the final distance and surfaced through a mass of slimy weeds that clung to my face. We were sheltered by chokecherry trees, with their shiny curved leaves.

At least I had on my tennis shoes and didn't have to feel the squishy mud between my toes. Sean popped his head up and glided over to me. "Hide over here in the weeds," I whispered.

Now for the wolverine. He continued to paddle lazily in the water, like a sunbather at Huntington Beach. But we had to hide him, too.

I stood, waist deep, water draining over me, and dug the tortillas out of my pockets. The baggies, luckily, had proved waterproof. I unzipped one and tossed a bit of tortilla on the water in front of the wolverine. The triangle of tortilla floated; the wolverine paddled over and gulped it down. The way to a wolverine's heart—

I tossed another and another until the wolverine was floating only a foot away from us. His mouth was slightly open, sucking in the last of the tortilla and water, like a whale sucking in krill through his baleen plates.

"Look at his teeth," whispered Sean. They were jagged points of white, frighteningly long now that we were so close.

From the fringe of trees near us came more crashing sounds, and dogs barked. Marshall and company were almost upon us.

I held out a piece of tortilla, praying: *Please, God, however you and Noah managed the animals, help me like that now.*

The wolverine glided up to me and neatly took the tortilla from my hand, his warm mouth touching my fingertips. He stared me in the eye, confident, unafraid. Around his neck was some kind of collar. A pet? Another crash made me pay attention. I ducked back down so that only my head was above water. Sean was nearly submerged, too.

More crashing—and three hounds appeared. Not the dobies he'd had in his truck, but large bloodhound-looking dogs.

Then he walked out of the trees. The great white hunter, with two of our burros. Mr. Marshall stopped at the muddy shore, opposite us and opposite the place the wolverine had sat. His dogs paced around him, sniffing. His rifle was slung over his shoulder; his ever-present cigarette curled smoke over his head.

I shivered, not from the cold water, and I sank lower, wishing the reedy grasses poking up in the water were even thicker. The wolverine glanced over at the man; his upper lip curled in a silent snarl. His big tail started to float out of the weeds, and without thinking I put my hand out and pulled his tail back into the shadows.

The wolverine swiveled his head to stare to me. His funny greenish-yellow eyes pierced me, but he didn't snarl or threaten.

The water lapped lightly against us. I shivered uncontrollably. The hounds panted loudly, snuffling around, but they didn't bay. The winds, which had been whirling overhead, blowing one way and then another, when we'd first found the pool, now blew steadily across the dogs and toward us, keeping them from scenting the wolverine. I wondered what God was thinking about all this—was he laughing or was he serious?

Finally, the great white hunter threw his cigarette down, stamped it, and moved on. He called the dogs with a shout, and they pushed through the bushes and out of the chokecherry trees. Our burros crashed about and muttered in coarse voices.

I smiled to myself, wondering if the burros were deliberately making noise, for they could walk silently when they wished.

123

The three of us stayed in the cold water for long minutes. Sean and I stayed just in case the great white hunter doubled back. I'm not sure why the wolverine stayed. Hoping for more handouts?

But then the wolverine grew impatient and pulled himself out, dripping. He rolled like a dog and fell to grooming himself with his tongue and claws.

"I touched him," I whispered to Sean as we too climbed out of the pool. My fingers still burned from his touch, even while the rest of me shivered from cold.

"He knew you were helping," said Sean.

I remembered a burro who'd injured himself. Mama had called the vet and when the vet drove up in his truck, the burro had brayed a full welcome. He had known the man would help him.

We wrung the water from our clothes as best we could and picked up our backpacks. I knelt and looked under the mahogany bush. The wolverine was still tidily grooming.

"Now what?" asked Sean.

I had memorized Uncle Hector's map; I flashed it out in my mind. Numbers I was no good at, but places I could remember. "We go northeast," I said. "To the wilderness area. And I've got more tortillas. Maybe he'll follow."

"Mr. Marshall will be coming back," said Sean. "Won't take him long to realize the trail ended here."

I twisted my hair and thought. The stream ran south, the way we'd come, and it appeared to come from a spring that seeped out from under a stone. So we couldn't walk upstream and disguise our scent.

"Maybe we can muddle the wolverine's tracks," said Sean. "You know, walk on them."

"Maybe." I didn't have any better ideas, except a wild one: Carry the wolverine. As if he'd let me. Letting me touch his tail wasn't quite an invitation to carry him.

"Let's go," I said. "We can't stay here." I dangled a tortilla in front of the wolverine. He raised his head and snapped it from my fingers. "Come on, buddy," I said. I held another piece out, and he scrambled from the mahogany bush and followed us.

The wolverine trotted behind us, beside us, in front of us. His tracks were all over the place. At first we tried to stamp them out, but we didn't want to waste time trying to get them all. Besides, we figured the dogs would scent the wolverine even through our scents.

But the wolverine stayed with us. I fed him pieces of tortilla, but I couldn't help thinking he stayed with us for more reasons than that.

Now if it would only rain and hide our scent and tracks completely. But the sky wasn't cooperating. The clouds were there, but playing hide-and-seek with the wind, darting around, stringing themselves out in long white threads. We hiked fast along a deer trail.

"He's gone," said Sean, suddenly.

"I just saw him back by that tree," I said, pointing to a big black oak.

We backtracked. His prints paraded merrily all over the place, then around the oak. I looked up. The wolverine was high above us, on a branch, swaying in the wind, his wedge-shaped head alert, listening.

We waited for the wolverine until he came back down. "What did you see?" I asked him.

He answered by breaking into a clumsy lope, and we wordlessly ran after him, knowing the answer.

The sun, despite the clouds, dried us out fast. As we ran, sweat began to pour down my backbone and made my skin itch. Behind us, blown sideways by the wind, was the sound of barking.

22
The Night of the Wolverine

Sean and I ran blindly after the wolverine—off the trail, through brush, over stones. I scratched my hand on a chamise bush, and a few drops of my blood spattered in the wind.

Even if we could reach it, the wilderness area wasn't necessarily a safe place. Sure, no hunting was allowed there, but that wouldn't stop the great white hunter.

Maybe I'd have to quit school and live up here, following the wolverine around to keep him safe. Maybe the wolverine would start bringing me food. I could see us sitting around together gnawing on rabbit bones.

The wolverine ran fast, in long, loping strides, heading north. Sean and I struggled after him. Surely Marshall's dogs would catch us soon. I pushed myself harder.

Depending on how far east we were, we might hit the wilderness area. But if we kept going straight north we'd hit the Angeles Crest Highway. Not good.

The three of us ran and ran. Sweat beaded on my face and ran into my eyes. My legs ached. My lungs burned. I was going to have to stop soon. But the wolverine rocked on, tireless and magnificent, his fur flattening in the wind.

Finally I had to walk. The stitch in my side was killing me. "I hate being a wimp," I said between pants.

"You're not a wimp," Sean said, throwing himself down on some mossy pine needles. "I'm dying, too."

I collapsed next to him. Let the great white hunter come. I couldn't breathe. We gasped for air together. We must have climbed another thousand feet or so; that would explain my bursting lungs. I was used to hiking and running, but at *two* thousand feet, not four or five thousand. After a few moments I sat up. The grove we'd collapsed in was quiet.

The wolverine had vanished. I hoped he had kept running, never to be seen again.

Sean rolled onto his back, looked at his wristwatch, and groaned. "My mother will kill me if I don't get back today," he said.

"What time is it?" I asked.

He held up his watch. One-twenty.

"You better go," I said.

He propped himself up on his elbow. "I can't leave you."

"Sure you can," I said. "Just walk away."

"Reba!"

"Sean!"

We glared at each other a long moment. The winds

128

shifted, cooler as they whipped around Vetter Mountain and Mount Pacifico in the north.

"If you don't go," I said, "your parents may never let you come here again."

He pushed up his glasses. "Okay," he said finally. "I'll go back and tell Uncle Hector. He can track you so you won't be alone."

I thought it over. I wouldn't like to spend the night without a sleeping bag, although at least I had my jacket. "All right," I said. "He'll come."

Sean gave me some food and a canteen from his pack. I was used to being alone in the mountains, but I'd never been this far in by myself. Except I wasn't really alone. There was the wolverine. And God. I squinted into the sky. *You are there, aren't you?*

Sean gave me a quick hug, which surprised me so much I nearly straight-armed him. Then he punched me lightly on the shoulder and took off trotting back the way we came.

When Sean was out of sight, I began searching for the wolverine's pawprints. I listened for dogs. Nothing. The winds were cooling now. The low, bushy chaparral turned their leaves away from the winds, protecting themselves. No such luck for me. I faced the teeth of the winds—and then I saw the wolverine's tracks.

He was moving north, straight into the wind, which didn't seem smart to me—the dogs would catch his scent that way.

The ground was sandy in spots; more tracks showed. I jumped low bushes and tore through brush after him. My hands and arms, getting more scratched, bled slow drops of blood.

Late in the afternoon I stopped to rest, leaning against a lump of rose quartz, clear and pink and lovely. I ate a packet of chicken and drank some water. I was so tired, more tired than I'd ever been before. I leaned my head against the rose quartz and sank into sleep, like a warm bath, sliding deeper and deeper—

—until something touched me.

I opened my eyes. He sat looking at me, head cocked, one paw with five claws on my knee.

"Hello," I said. What else do you say to a wild wolverine?

He removed his paw and licked it, then washed his face, like a cat. Well, my mother would be glad he was clean. I almost laughed out loud.

His whiskers were sturdy and wiry, but his face looked soft and young. I touched his furry ruff. His collar was thick nylon and had a black square on it. He didn't move, so I sank my fingers into his coarse outer fur, then into the soft underfur.

He sat very still, his eyes on mine, as if he was asking me something. I think he knew my answer.

Then the barking flooded the sky.

The wolverine pulled back and stood, nose up. He twitched his tail delicately.

There was so much more I wanted to know. Why had the wolverine come here, why had he trashed the cabins, why—

But now he sprang into a run again, and I jumped after him. Sometimes he led, sometimes I led. I tried to head east, for the wilderness, but he aimed more north—thinking of the welcome, vibrant cold of his world, no doubt.

We threaded our way between sharp mesquite, grease-wood, and stunted knobcone pines; we crawled over gritty granite lumps. The sky darkened, red flames and gold sparks dying out among the dark silhouettes of tree branches. The night spread out, thick and heavy as tar.

The winds slowed to a breath; the night held still, waiting.

Seeing only by the scatter of stars, I followed the wolverine now. How I longed for animal sight, animal senses. I kept banging my shins on rocks and dropping suddenly into depressions, jarring my legs and hips. Once I fell and hit my chin. Blood trickled down my neck. But we kept on, walking, jogging.

I thought maybe this was how the rest of my life would be. Walking and following the wolverine wherever he led. But I wanted to do this, I had chosen it, so it was all right.

A fine, thin moon rose. Our progress picked up. It occurred to me that I was slowing the wolverine down, but he patiently waited for me to catch up. Always trotting north. I could see Polaris, the North Star, winking.

Finally we stopped to rest in a hollow chosen by the wolverine. He curled up, nose on tail. I did almost the same, bending my spine, nose to knees, wishing I had a tail to keep my nose warm. I shivered from exhaustion.

"I don't even know your name," I whispered.

He stirred at my voice, then gave a very human-sounding sigh. I reached out and sank my fingers in his fur. He was warm, soft. I shifted closer until I lay twined in his fur. The moon vanished into clouds, and we slept in deep shadows.

23
Up
in a
Tree

An animal was licking my cheek. I opened my eyes. The sky was grey, mushy—dawn. That silly wolverine. Licking my face. I yawned. I opened my eyes, sat up, and looked into the eyes of a dog.

Dog! I leaped to my feet, backing up, my heart pounding. It was one of the great white hunter's dogs. A hound with floppy ears and loose skin. The hound from hell. Except that he had licked my face, and he was wagging his tail.

The dog whined gently and sniffed where I'd been

lying. Frantically, I searched the swaying sugar pines and black oaks. But the wolverine didn't seem to be overhead.

The morning winds hissed through the needles and leaves, much cooler and smelling of damp things. The hound whined again and pressed his nose into my hand. Then he lifted his snout, opened his mouth and bayed—*whooo-whoo*, like a lost train.

I snatched my hand back as if he'd burnt me. Maybe he had. "You're not here to help me," I said, feeling sick. I grabbed my backpack and ran.

Of course the hound ran after me, his ears flopping back, his voice rising above the wail of the winds. *Whooo-whoo*. Now I knew: I had to lead them away from the wolverine. So I turned my back to the sun and ran west, flying around old manzanita bushes and leaping over rose quartz and granite.

But the hounds were faster. They caught up to me before I'd gotten very far. In the distance, Strawberry Peak nosed out of the mushy clouds. Three tan, floppy-eared dogs circled me, like wolves, baying through their teeth that gleamed in the morning light.

I put my hands over my ears. What a noise! Any animal caught by these hounds would be terrified.

I prayed the wolverine had gone far, far away.

I tried to step out of the circle of hounds, but they lifted flaps of jowls, showing the outline of each sharp tooth in snarled warnings. So I stood in their circle, waiting.

The wind blew steadily from the north now. I turned my back to the cold, facing south now—and saw him. The wolverine. He watched me from up a black oak. *No*, I mouthed—*No. Run!*

Two dogs, wagging their tails now, turned and looked away from me, toward the great white hunter, who hadn't yet appeared in the clearing. The third, the one who had found me, stared at me—then, a crafty dog, an experienced hunter who knew how to read his prey, turned slowly, slowly to face the direction I had looked. His hackles rose.

No.

He gave a huge bark and rushed the black oak. The wolverine growled down deep.

"Run!" I burst out, hopeless. How could he outrun these dogs now? The first hound danced on his hind legs, barking up at the wolverine, who puffed up his neck fur and snarled like an enormous cat.

The great white hunter came over the hill with the pack burros. When the burros saw me they brayed a welcome.

"Idiot!" Mr. Marshall yelled, his voice like a gunshot. "You little fool!"

I broke past the hounds and ran for the wolverine's tree. They rushed up behind me as I grabbed hold of the tree branch closest to the ground and swung up. One of them leaped for the same branch, his front paws scrabbling for a hold. I kicked him in the jaw. He yelped and fell back the ground. Then he rebounded, snarling and snapping, but I was higher now, away from his jaws. My arms ached as I climbed, recklessly fast, until I straddled the branch the wolverine clung to. The wolverine continued snarling at the dogs.

Then Mr. Marshall appeared under the tree and lit a cigarette. The acrid smell stung my nostrils, and the wolverine snarled louder.

Mr. Marshall called the dogs off, yanking them back by their collars, silencing them. He pulled them over one by one to the pack burros and snapped ropes to their collars. The hounds sulked as the burros shied away from the dogs.

Slowly the wolverine's fur went down. Again I had the thought of gathering the wolverine in my arms and carrying him—where? Away. To a safe place. But where was that?

Finished with the dogs, Mr. Marshall unstrapped his rifle from the burro's pack.

I swallowed. Hard.

"Come down, Reba," said the great white hunter. "Let's not play around."

Mama's words rang back to me: "Don't get in his way."

But here I was. In his way. I'm sorry, Mama. No, he's in *my* way.

"*Now*, Reba," he said.

At his voice, the wolverine, never taking his eyes off the man, sat down on the broad branch. A hound barked sharply.

I shook my head. I would not. Could not.

In fact, I—

—I stretched my hand out and touched the wolverine's plush side. He jumped, then gave me an inscrutable look. I didn't remove my hand. He allowed my fingers to dwell in his deep, dark fur.

"Don't be crazy, girl," Mr. Marshall said softly, unbelieving. "That animal will shred you!"

But his words only gave me courage.

I slipped back along the branch so that my back was pressed against the solid tree trunk. I leaned back for security, my legs dangling on either side of the branch.

The wolverine spat at the hunter and ended the hiss in a loud growl. The hounds growled back. Then the wolverine walked three steps to me and sat between my legs, his back to me. I put my arms around him, his fur so deep and soft.

The wolverine sat like a pet. No, like a friend, a companion. I let my hand run down his strong back. He leaned into my hand.

"We're not coming down," I said.

Mr. Marshall stood directly under our branch.

"Okay, girl," he said. "Enough of this. Down."

"No." I think the wolverine and I said the word together.

"Then I'll just have to shoot him out from under you."

24
A Safe Place

I don't believe that would be a good idea," said Uncle Hector's voice. Then, like magic, Uncle Hector was there, sitting on his medicine hat horse, one old hand on the rein, the other on his horse's white mane. I started to tremble and the wolverine pressed closer to me.

The great white hunter started, then said over his shoulder, in an awful, fake-innocent tone, "I wouldn't really. You know that."

Sure you wouldn't. The wolverine nuzzled my arm for a moment, his breath hot. He knew the truth, too.

"Now, Reba, honey, come on down," said the great white hunter.

Honey?

I settled in deeper.

Uncle Hector rode the medicine hat horse past the hunter and his dogs. The horse blew loudly, not liking the wolverine scent. But Uncle Hector coaxed his horse up under us. The great white hunter moved away. One of the dogs began whining, like air being let out of a tire.

"You okay?" Uncle Hector asked me, softly. "I'm sorry I couldn't find you last night, *mi hija*. Your tracks were like *la hada*, a fairy."

"It's all right," I said, my fingers still deep in the wolverine's fur. The wolverine stopped growling and stared down at Uncle Hector and his hatted horse.

"You just stay there. No hurry," he said, a wicked sparkle in his eyes. "Pretty soon we'll have some more company."

"What does that mean?" said Mr. Marshall.

"That means Reba mailed a letter to *The Pasadena Star News* telling the reporters about this situation," said Uncle Hector, brushing back his greying hair. "And I did some calling around yesterday afternoon with Maury. It seems this wolverine is being monitored by biologists. Have you heard of endangered animals, Mr. Marshall?"

My fingers touched the collar. A radio collar!

Mr. Marshall frowned, almost snarling. "See here—I'm just trying to do my job and get rid of that animal."

"Seems to me," I said, "that you've done your job. The wolverine isn't near the construction area anymore."

"That animal is dangerous! How can you guarantee he won't be back?" asked Mr. Marshall.

Dangerous? I thought of Mr. Bentley's cabin, and knew that I couldn't argue with that. He didn't belong around people. "If there *is* trouble with him again, Mr. Marshall, I'll help."

"And," added Uncle Hector, "the biologists would like to know about him."

Mr. Marshall started to say something, but a rumble interrupted him.

The reporters and biologists in a helicopter? I squinted and looked up into the mushy sky. Something cold hit me square between the eyes.

Rain.

Slowly the huge drops fell into the dust, leaving soft pockmarks. The burros opened their mouths and caught the rain on their tongues.

I whispered to the wolverine, "You're safe. They can't track you in the rain."

His ear twitched. I petted his round head. He sat for a moment, as if considering my words—and then leaped off the branch, down the trunk and away, heading north—darn him!—like a flicker of black lightning.

I sat on the branch, in the rain. The drops slid through the many leaves and pinged me over and over.

Uncle Hector's voice called, "Come down, Reba."

Something big moved into my vision, above the trees. The helicopter. The great white hunter swore.

Slowly, I slid down from the tree, and the helicopter landed on a near ridge that was bare and wide enough. The helicopter perched on the mountain like a monstrous insect, vibrating, roaring with energy. Two men hopped out, one packed with camera equipment.

"By God," yelled the one with the camera. "We saw the wolverine running. Got some terrific shots, I think."

By God. Yes, maybe it was by God.

The reporters rushed to Mr. Marshall, cameras and tape recorders ready. Another man, a biologist, asked, "Did you know that wolverines are almost extinct in North America?"

But Mr. Marshall turned away, shaking his head like a balky burro. "No comment." He gathered up his dogs and our burros. *He'd better not hurt them*, I thought.

139

I gripped Uncle Hector's arm. "I'm glad you found me."

"Me, too. Now climb up." I put my foot in the stirrup and swung up behind Uncle Hector. He'd folded a saddle blanket over his horse's flanks, and I sat with my arms around his waist.

Uncle Hector clucked, and the medicine hat horse started home.

"Wait, wait!" The reporters ran after us. The camera shutter clicked madly, making the horse shy.

"I've got to get this girl back," called Uncle Hector. "Meet us at Chantry Flat." He kicked the medicine hat horse into a trot and we jogged away. Over my shoulder, I watched the reporters, still yelling, and the noisy helicopter with its whirling blades fade into the curtain of water.

The rain was cold, but not too cold. And I didn't mind. After all, it was four years since it had rained.

We rode a long time. I think I fell asleep, bobbing against Uncle Hector.

When we reached Uncle Hector's house, the sky frowned, dark and rainy. I slid off and leaned against the barn door. Uncle Hector carefully put the medicine hat horse in the barn, drying him with old towels. The barn still smelled like a wolverine. Then Uncle Hector and I walked to his cabin, stepping over small streams of water. Water.

A light from his cabin shone through the rainy darkness.

We opened the door and Mama was inside.

"Reba." Mama took me wet in her arms.

"She's fine," said Uncle Hector. "Just fine."

I looked up. Mama had rain on her face. No—tears.

"I worried over you," she said, and sniffed.

If I love an animal—a wolverine, a wild beast—that I hardly know, I thought, *then how much more do I love Mama, who loves me back, even though it doesn't always seem like it.* How selfish I had been—and probably would be again. But at least I could *try* to change, with God helping me.

I closed my eyes and imagined the wolverine, flinging himself along in the rain, splashing through muddy puddles, laughing to himself because the rain fouled his trail and no one would track him now.

Keep heading north, my friend. To a safe place.

I hugged Mama tighter.